# THE COLOUR OF THE SEA

# THE COLOUR
# OF THE SEA

BY

## ROSEMARY HAMMOND

**MILLS & BOON LIMITED**
ETON HOUSE  18–24 PARADISE ROAD
RICHMOND  SURREY  TW9 1SR

First published in Great Britain 1985
by Mills & Boon Limited

© Rosemary Hammond 1985

Australian copyright 1985
Philippine copyright 1991
This edition 1991

ISBN 0 263 77309 4

Set in Linotron Times 11 on 12 pt.
97-9108-46,150

Made and printed in Great Britain

# CHAPTER ONE

'You're sure you're okay, then, Laurie?' the tall fair-haired young man asked.

Laurie smiled up at him from the doorway of the cottage. 'Yes, Ted,' she said patiently. 'Please don't worry about me. I'll be fine.'

Still, a frown marred the pleasant symmetry of his regular features. 'I can't help it,' he said softly, 'I do.' He leaned towards her. 'If only you'd marry me . . .' he began.

Laurie turned her head away. 'Please, Ted,' she sighed, 'we've been all over this before. It's too soon to think of anything like that.'

Ted straightened up, his lips tight. 'Laurie, your father has been dead for three months now. Surely that's long enough to mourn?' He made an impatient gesture with his hand towards the narrow bronze plaque nailed up beside the front door. 'James C. Cochran, MD—Look, you haven't even taken down his shingle yet.'

Laurie looked up at him, her clear grey eyes half hidden beneath the thick fringe of long black lashes. 'You don't understand,' she said firmly. 'It's not just that.'

How could she explain to him? she thought to herself as she watched the exasperated look on his good, kind face turn to petulance. How could she

5

tell him that she just didn't love him enough, or in the right way, to marry him? That she didn't want to marry anyone?

He sighed and shrugged his shoulders.

'Okay, okay,' he said, 'I'll quit pushing.' He managed to force a weak smile. 'We'll be up in Alaska fishing at Bristol Bay for about a month, then, if the weather holds, go on up to the Bering Sea. We should be back before Christmas, hopefully with a big catch. The Bendiksens at the hotel will look after you, you know that.'

'I know, Ted,' Laurie said with a smile. She felt perfectly capable of looking after herself. 'Good fishing!'

They said goodbye, then, and she stood at the door and watched him as he walked down the winding path that led away from the house until finally the clump of birch and wild profusion of shrubbery hid him from view.

Laurie heaved a deep sigh, half of regret to see him go, half of relief, and went back into the house. She walked down the long hallway that led from the front door through the length of the house to the back. On the right was her father's old consulting room and surgery, sterile, spotless, with gleaming chrome, white enamel, and his diplomas hung on the pale yellow wall.

She turned to the left, into the small parlour that had served as a waiting room. She walked to the window that overlooked the rocky beach below and the wide expanse of the Haro Straits, with the huge land mass of Vancouver Island in the distance.

Even though Laurie had been born and grown up in the San Juan Islands, that gem-like cluster set like emeralds in the blue sea between Vancouver Island on the west and Washington state on the east, the view from this window never failed to make her catch her breath in sheer delight.

It was early fall, almost October, and although the towering firs, pine, hemlock and cedar never changed their dark green colour, the graceful vine maple and sumac were just beginning to take on a reddish tinge, the birch a flame of gold.

Down on the beach she could see Ted walking back to his own place, about a quarter of a mile north. His blond head gleamed in the morning sun, and she wondered for the thousandth time if she wasn't being foolish not to marry him.

Although he was twenty-five—four years older than Laurie—they had grown up together on the tiny island of Cadranelle, where there were so few children a four-year age gap was insignificant.

She ran a hand through the silky smooth black hair, so fine and thick that it seemed like a dark cap falling softly around the fine-boned sensitive face.

It was early afternoon, still time, she decided, to get some painting done. She ran upstairs to get a sweater. A breeze usually sprang up later in the afternoon, chilling the air, and she only had on a pair of lightweight poplin pants and a cotton shirt.

She kept her painting things in a small closet at the back of the ground floor of the cottage. Outside there was a small enclosure, protected by a thicket of wild blackberries, huckleberries and broom. It was on the north side of the house, giving her the best light.

She set up her easel and got out her paints, then tacked up the canvas she had been working on, a full-length portrait of her father, with the sea as background.

Every time she got the picture out, tears would come to her eyes again when she saw the familiar face and form. How dear he had been to her! How much she missed him and the pleasant life they had had together. It still seemed to her that she would hear his step on the stair, the kind teasing voice, that any minute he might suddenly reappear.

She sat down on her camp stool, squinting at the picture. Luckily she had finished the actual portrait before he died, but she couldn't get the background right. She wanted so badly to capture that distinctive colour of the straits at full tide, a deep metallic blue with a tinge of green, but she could never get it quite right on canvas the way she envisaged it in her mind's eye.

By four o'clock a strong wind had come up from the straits, bringing with it a mass of black clouds to obscure the sun, and she had to quit. There were whitecaps on the water, and the angry surf foamed and crashed up against the jagged outcropping of rock that lined the shore.

As she packed up her painting gear she thought about Ted and his father out in the chop on their boat. They were both good sailors, and with luck would have made it up to Vancouver on the British Columbia mainland by now. The fall winds could be very treacherous out on the open sea, and they had to get across the wide Straits of Georgia before dark.

She checked to make sure all the downstairs windows and doors were fastened tight before going up to the living quarters on the second floor.

She still felt a pang of sorrow whenever she entered her father's consulting room. As the only doctor in the northern part of the San Juans, he had had a busy practice, his patients coming by boat from all the tiny islands nearby. They were mostly fishermen or sheep ranchers and their families, silent hard-working people who often paid their low bills with a fresh catch of salmon or a side of spring lamb or a bucket of crab, and although little money actually came in, the freezer was always full.

As she went upstairs, Laurie wondered if she should venture out and have dinner with the Bendiksens at the small hotel at the crest of the island. After Labor Day, when all the tourists had gone home, the hotel became the evening gathering place for the natives, and Laurie was especially grateful for the familiar company now that her father was gone.

A sudden gust of wind rattled the windowpanes, and the rain began to beat against them in a torrent. So much for the hotel, she thought, as she went around securing the upstairs windows. Better not get caught out in that storm.

It was dark by now. She switched on the lights and lit a fire in the large room that served as living room, dining room and library. The kitchen, separated from the main room by an island counter, was at one end so that she could enjoy the fire while she had her dinner.

She turned on the radio to listen to the evening weather report. There were gale warnings out in the Straits of Juan de Fuca, that miles-wide channel in from the Pacific Ocean. The islands were somewhat sheltered by the enormous protecting bulk of Vancouver Island, but still felt the sting of those terrible fall storms, near hurricane force.

As the evening progressed, the wind howled and screamed around the house, whistling in through all the chinks and rattling the windows. Laurie felt restless.

She knew there was no real danger. The cottage was sound and built up on a rise high enough to escape the thunderous waves raised by the storm. Still, the sound of it was unnerving, and she did worry that one of the huge fir trees surrounding the wooden frame house might come crashing down on it, crushing it.

Her father used to comfort her by telling her that those trees, all virgin forest, had probably been there hundreds of years and withstood worse storms.

She tried to read, but couldn't concentrate. The weather report had predicted a mild period starting tomorrow after the storm blew over, but right now it seemed as though the gates of hell had opened to pour out their fury.

Finally she decided to take a bath, get into bed, and try once again to read. She had undressed and was on her way into the bathroom to run her water in the tub when she heard a sudden loud banging from outside. She listened, alarmed. It came again. It sounded as though a heavy branch might have broken off a tree in the wind and blown against the house.

The noise came again. Worried that it might do some real damage to the house, Laurie slipped on a short silky robe, black with large red poppies, tied it securely at the waist, and went downstairs.

As she padded down the hall in her bare feet, she heard it again, this time feebler. It seemed to be coming from the front of the house, as though a branch had lodged itself in one of the cracks between the floorboards of the front porch and was beating against the door.

She turned on the porch light, unlocked the heavy oak door, and pulled it open. A sudden gust of wind almost knocked her down. The noise from the storm was terrific, the huge waves crashing on the rocks below, the violent wind soughing through the trees. She put an arm up to protect her head and peered out.

At first she could only see the turbulence of the storm out in the dark night, but as she glanced around the porch, something, a slight movement, caught her eye. She looked again. There, to one side in the shadows, leaning up against the house, was a man. Laurie gasped and backed away, startled, instinctively retreating. All she could think about was to get inside and slam the door shut against the intruder.

There were few strangers on the little island at this time of year. She had glimpsed his face and hadn't recognised him. Fear had made her back off, but curiosity made her hesitate. She looked at him again.

He had moved slightly so that now he was standing just under the porch light. His face was white and drawn, and he leaned against the house as though he would not have been able to stand alone. He was clutching his left arm with his right hand, and on closer look, Laurie could see blood on the hand. He was soaked to the skin, his dark hair plastered across his forehead.

She heard him mutter weakly. 'Doctor. Hurt.'

Oh, Lord, she thought, he's been hurt and come here looking for a doctor. What should she do? How could she tell him there was no doctor here any more? Where could she send him? She hesitated, then remembered that she was a doctor's daughter and made her decision.

'Come inside,' she said. She stepped out on to the porch and took hold of his good arm, supporting him, pulling him along with her gently. The wind whipped the skirt of her robe around her legs, and although the porch was covered, she could feel the driving rain beginning to soak through her thin robe.

'Come,' she urged, and pulled harder.

Slowly he straightened up and gave her a dazed look, then began to shuffle haltingly towards the door, leaning some of his weight on her arm.

Once inside, Laurie shut the door against the

violence of the storm and turned to look at him more closely. Her fear had vanished by now. He was obviously badly hurt and had probably lost some blood. His clothes were torn and dripping wet, and a small puddle began to form on the floor at his feet.

Supporting him with an arm around his waist, she let him into her father's old surgery. He was a large man, quite tall, and although he seemed to be making every effort to manoeuvre under his own steam, Laurie barely had the strength to get him inside the surgery.

Laurie had never had any formal nurse's training, but her mother had been a nurse, and until she died, six years ago, had taught Laurie enough so that when she was gone Laurie was able to assist her father in everything from giving shots to delivering babies and emergency surgery. There was no hospital on Cadranelle, and the doctor's surgery had been the scene of many bone-settings, wound-stitchings and even an appendectomy or two.

Now Laurie eased the tall man down in a chair. He groaned and leaned his head back. He closed his eyes and seemed for a moment to have lost consciousness. Laurie got a towel from the linen cupboard and began to dry the thick black hair, the long white face.

As she leaned over him, tending him, he opened his eyes again and looked up straight into hers. Laurie caught her breath. The colour of his eyes was the most unusual she had ever seen. At first they had just seemed very dark, perhaps brown, but now, on closer look, she could see that they were a deep blue-green, a teal blue, just the colour of the sea.

There was brandy in the medicine cabinet, and she poured a glass and put it to his lips. As he sipped slowly, the colour began to return to his face and he seemed a little stronger.

'Sorry to barge in on you like this,' he said at last. His voice, although halting, was low and clear. 'I was out in the dinghy and got caught in the storm. Ran up against some rocks and got battered around a little.'

He looked down at his arm and slowly lifted the hand that had grasped it. Blood began to ooze slowly from a jagged gash, and he turned pale again.

'It's all right,' Laurie said quickly. 'It's only a vein—arteries spurt. Here, let's get your shirt off and I'll take a look at it.'

He leaned his head back again and watched under half-closed eyes as Laurie unbuttoned the drenched white shirt and pulled it off his good shoulder.

'Here,' she said, 'lean forward a little.'

He did so, and she pulled the shirt gently around his back and down over his injured arm. She got a fresh towel and began to dry his arms, shoulders and chest. As she worked over him, she suddenly began to feel shy. The man was all bone and hard muscle, and when her fingers occasionally came in direct contact with his smooth skin, it was like a charge of electricity.

Although Laurie had helped her father tend many men, somehow this one seemed different. In spite of his weakened condition, she sensed unleashed power in those broad shoulders and hard chest muscles. He seemed dangerous, threatening in a way she didn't understand.

'Are you the doctor?' he asked. There was a hint of mockery in his tone.

'No,' she said sharply, straightening up. 'My father is—was—the doctor. He's dead.'

She examined the gash in his arm. It would need stitches. His chest and back were covered with scratches and bruises. There were most likely no bones broken or he wouldn't have been able to make it up from the beach to the house under his own steam, especially in the storm.

'That arm is going to need stitches to stop the bleeding,' she said. 'The nearest doctor is in Friday Harbor, and there's no way you can get there until tomorrow.'

He thought this over. 'Can you do it?' he asked.

'The stitching? I've done it before and watched many times.' She gazed directly into those startling eyes. 'It's up to you.'

He gave her a weak smile. 'You're very direct,' he said. 'Okay, I'm in your hands.'

Laurie covered the surgery table with a clean sheet and helped him up on to it. He lay down on his back and closed his eyes, obviously exhausted.

She worked quickly, rubbing a cotton pad soaked in antiseptic all over the powerful chest and lean muscular arms. She knew it must sting badly, and although she saw him wince a few times, he didn't utter a sound.

'I can't give you any anaesthetic for the stitches,' she said grimly. 'Not allowed to. How about some more brandy?'

He opened his eyes and gazed up at her leaning over him. He smiled, and his eyes left her face to travel downwards.

Suddenly, for the first time, it dawned on her that all she had on was that thin silk robe, secured only by a hastily-tied belt that had come loose from her struggles to get the man inside and was now, she assumed, gaping open enough on top so that a good portion of her full firm breast was visible to those penetrating eyes.

She quickly straightened up and gathered the robe more tightly around her, tying it securely, realising, however, as she did so, that what lay underneath the robe was only more sharply outlined.

She poured another glass of brandy, propped his head up with her arm, and held the glass to his lips. 'Here,' she said, 'this will help. I think two stitches will do it. It'll be quick anyway.'

It was over in less than a minute. So concentrated on her work that she forgot all about the man as a person, Laurie didn't realise that he had lost consciousness until she had finished bandaging his arm.

She stood gazing down at him. The shock of his injuries, the struggle to get ashore and up to the house, plus the brandy, had finally taken their toll.

He had lost a lot of blood. His face was drained of colour underneath a heavy tan.

He must be in mild shock, she thought. I've got to get him into a warm bed. She glanced down at his black trousers, still soaking wet. What should she do? Cover him up here and hope he didn't fall off in the night? She'd have to take his wet trousers off. Could she rouse him, get him upstairs and into bed somehow?

As she gazed at him, it occurred to her for the first time that this was an intensely attractive man. His hair had dried now and fell in soft thick waves over his forehead, curled around his ears. His face was long, with prominent cheekbones and flat planes leading down to a strong jaw. His black lashes were thick on his cheeks, the heavy eyebrows almost meeting in the centre. The nose was straight and strong, the mouth firm, but with a full, sensuous underlip.

He stirred and opened his eyes.

'How do you feel?' asked Laurie.

'It hurts like hell,' he muttered.

She smiled. 'I know—I'm sorry. I'll give you some aspirin. I'm not allowed to dispense anything stronger. Do you think you can manage to get upstairs? You should get those wet clothes off and get into bed. You need to sleep.'

He smiled weakly. 'I can but try,' he said.

She helped him to sit up, and although he swayed a little, he seemed to be able to maintain his equilibrium. She grasped him firmly around the waist and with his good arm around her shoulders, gently helped him slide off the table onto the floor.

Slowly, leaning heavily on her, he finally did make it up the stairs. Laurie took him into her father's old bedroom and guided him to the bed.

'Do you think you can get undressed by yourself?' she asked. 'I'll get you a pair of my father's pyjamas.'

He gave her an amused look. 'I'm very sorry to say that there isn't the faintest chance I can get these clothes off by myself,' he announced. 'So either you'll have to help me, or I'll have to get into bed with wet trousers.'

'Are you making fun of me?' she asked suspiciously.

He sighed. 'My dear girl, I really don't have the strength to play games.'

He swayed a little, then, and she reached out to support him. He really was still quite weak, she thought.

'All right, then,' she said. 'I guess I don't have a choice.' She set her mouth in a line of grim determination and reached down to unbuckle his belt.

Then she felt one of his hands on hers.

'Tell you what,' he said. 'Get me a towel and wrap it around my waist. I've got to get dried anyway.'

With a sigh of relief, she did as he suggested. With a large towel securely covering his lower body, she found it a simple matter to undo his trousers and pull them down around his feet.

She helped him on with the pyjama jacket, leaving it unbuttoned because it was far too small for him, and with the towel still around his waist, he sank heavily on to the bed.

She took off his shoes and socks, then covered him up. After she had picked up his wet clothes and carried them into the bathroom, she brought him some aspirin and a glass of water, then she sat down on the bed and held his head up while he swallowed them.

Then he sank his head back on the pillow and looked up at her. A little colour had come back into his face and he seemed to be relaxed.

'Thank you, angel of mercy,' he murmured. 'I don't even know your name.'

'It's Laurie,' she said. 'Laurie Cochran.'

'Laurie,' he repeated softly. Then he closed his eyes.

Laurie turned off the light and quietly went out of the room, leaving the door ajar in case he called out during the night.

She put on her nightgown and slipped into bed. She lay there in the dark listening to the storm still crashing about the house, thinking about the strange man in the bedroom across the hall.

Who was he? Where had he come from? What was there about him that she found so unnerving, so threatening—and, she had to admit, so compelling?

During the night the storm finally abated. The sudden silence woke Laurie up. She got out of bed and went to the window, pulling the curtain aside.

There was a dazzling moon, with only a few wisps of clouds remaining in the midnight blue sky. The tree branches glistened from the raindrops still clinging to them like jewels. From the straits she heard the screeching of the seagulls, the pounding of the surf. Her heart was filled with the peace that comes after a storm and love of this place that was her home.

Then, with a little shock, she remembered the man lying in her father's bed. She walked softly across the hall and looked inside the bedroom, almost surprised to find that he was still there.

The moon shone dimly through the thin curtains, outlining his form under the bedclothes. He was as she had left him, his dark head on the pillow turned towards her, his arms outside the covers, lying at his sides.

She tiptoed over to the bed and looked down at him. In repose, his eyes closed, the heavy dark lashes lying on the high cheekbones, the mouth relaxed, he looked to her like a prince out of a fairy tale, a hero, almost a god.

She put a hand on his forehead. It felt a little warm. There was always the danger of infection in these kinds of injuries. Some time had necessarily elapsed before they were properly cleaned. She held his wrist. The pulse seemed steady, perhaps a little fast.

Laurie went back to bed. She knew from experience that tomorrow would tell what his condition was. There was nothing more she could do for him tonight. What he needed most of all was rest, to get his strength back.

\* \* \*

The next morning Laurie was awakened by the sun streaming in through her bedroom window. She glanced at the clock on the bedside table. It was seven-thirty. She jumped out of bed and ran to the window.

The straits were still and calm, the tide moving in slowly on to the rocky beach in gentle undulating waves. The sky was a clear blue, and the immense evergreens that surrounded the cottage sparkled in the pale sunlight.

She felt a little thrill of excited apprehension when she remembered the strange man in the house. She glanced in at him on her way to the bathroom. He looked as though he hadn't moved.

She had hung his wet clothes up to dry on the shower curtain rod over the bathtub last night, and it gave her a shock to see the black trousers and white shirt there now. They were almost dry. She took them down and put them in the laundry hamper. Later she would wash and try to mend them.

Quickly she showered and dressed in a clean pair of blue denims and a checkered shirt. She knew she had to wake him in case he had a mild concussion, and she should take his temperature. He really ought to eat something, too.

She got out a thermometer from the medicine chest in the bathroom, washed it and shook it down, then went into his room. She sat down on the edge of the bed and watched him for several moments.

He was still deeply asleep, his breathing regular

and steady. Somehow during the night the too-small pyjama top had come off. As she sat there gazing at the strong arm and shoulder muscles, the long column of his neck, the dark hair tousled over his forehead, he seemed to her like some powerful animal that was in her care.

He looked so vulnerable in sleep, she thought, but the strength was there in the set of his jaw, the muscled body, only half covered by the bedclothes. There were tiny lines at the corners of his eyes.

She wondered again who he was, where he came from. He was certainly not a boy. How old was he? Not yet forty, she guessed, but not as young as thirty. It was hard to tell.

As she reached out a hand to shake him gently by the shoulder, he suddenly stirred. His eyes opened, blinked, then fastened their steady gaze on her.

Once again she was startled by those deep blue-green eyes. He smiled weakly and raised his good arm to rest it on his forehead.

'How do you feel?' Laurie asked softly.

He raised his head up to glance down at his injured arm, then winced and lay back on the pillow again, grimacing.

'Outside of a hell of a headache, an arm that hurts like the devil and a body that feels as though it had been put through a wringer, I feel quite well, thank you.'

She grinned. At least he had a sense of humour. He couldn't be too badly hurt.

'Are you hungry?' she asked.

He thought this over. 'Not really,' he replied. 'But I do have a raging thirst.'

She popped the thermometer into his mouth. 'I think you might have a fever,' she said. She took his wrist between her fingers to count his pulse. It was still fast.

When she read the thermometer, it registered a fever two degrees above normal. Not too bad, she thought, but definitely an indication of infection.

'Are you allergic to penicillin?' she asked. 'I'm afraid you have an infection.'

He raised a heavy dark eyebrow. 'No, I'm not allergic to penicillin,' he said. 'If I have an infection, does it mean I can sue you for malpractice?'

She laughed. 'Hardly, since I'm not a doctor. However, I suppose you could turn me in for practising medicine without a licence. That is, if you live.'

'Thanks a lot,' he said wryly. 'I like your bedside manner.'

Laurie stood up. 'I'm not surprised you're not hungry, but you really should try to eat something. I'll get some orange juice and coffee and make you some toast. Do you think you can navigate to the bathroom? It's just across the hall.'

'I'll try,' he said grimly.

She went downstairs to get some penicillin tablets, then came back up to the kitchen. She could hear water running in the bathroom as she passed down the hall. It was a good sign if he could get around on his own.

In ten minutes she had a tray ready for him and

carried it down the hall to his bedroom. He was sitting up in bed, his head propped back on the pillows. He looked drawn.

She set the tray down on the bedside table and handed him the glass of orange juice and a penicillin tablet.

'You look worn out,' she said. 'Take this, then try to sleep some more.'

He took the pill and drank the juice, but refused the toast and coffee. By then, his eyes had started to close again. Laurie guessed that the effort of getting up had exhausted him.

He watched her through half-shut eyes as she examined the dressing on his arm. It looked all right, she thought, no sign of bleeding. She'd have to examine the wound and change the dressing later.

She fixed his pillow so that he could lie down and gently eased him back by the shoulders. He was burning up. 'Sleep now,' she said gently, smoothing the hair back from his damp forehead. 'The penicillin takes a while to work. I'll be back later.'

He closed his eyes, and she left the room.

Laurie spent the rest of the morning washing his clothes and cleaning up the surgery. She looked in on him several times. He seemed more restless, tossing about in his fever, disturbing the bed-clothes.

As she covered him for the third time, she could tell that his fever had gone up. She wondered if she should try to get Dr Finney up from Friday Harbor, but she knew that was hopeless. Even if he was able and willing to come, it would take two hours to drive up to the northern end of San Juan Island on the badly rutted road, if it wasn't washed out by the storm, and another hour to cross the channel between the big island and Cadranelle by boat.

If he wasn't better by tomorrow, she decided, she would call Dr Finney in Friday Harbor and at least get his advice. In a real emergency they could always send up a seaplane or helicopter.

At noon she brought him a large glass of orange juice and another penicillin tablet. He was so weak from fever by now that she had to hold his head and put the tablet in his mouth, the glass to his lips.

By late afternoon his fever had gone higher. Every hour she came in to bathe his face, his shoulders and chest with cool water. She changed the dressing on his arm in the early evening. It looked all right. There was no red streaking from the wound, and the stitches were holding.

She sat up with him all night, dozing lightly in the chair by his bed, bathing him periodically and forcing penicillin and juice into his mouth every four hours.

Finally, towards morning, he seemed quieter, and she curled up in the armchair, falling, exhausted, into a deep sleep.

When she awoke, her muscles aching from the cramped position she had slept in, sunshine was streaming into the room. She glanced quickly at the man in the bed. He was sleeping peacefully.

She crossed over to him and felt his forehead. It was cool and damp. Thank God, she thought, the fever had broken. His colour was better. Now, if I can just get some food down him . . .

Suddenly his eyes opened and he gazed blankly up at her, obviously disorientated. Laurie leaned over him.

'How do you feel?' she asked.

He grinned weakly, a light of recognition dawning in the deep blue-green eyes. 'That's the same question you asked me yesterday,' he said. 'It was yesterday, wasn't it?'

She smiled back at him. 'Yes,' she replied, 'only yesterday.'

He raised himself up on his good elbow and gave her a more penetrating look. She was suddenly intensely aware of how she must look, her hair tousled, no make-up on, her clothes rumpled from the night in the chair.

'You sat up all night with me, didn't you?' he asked in a low voice.

She ran her fingers through her hair in an effort to make herself more presentable. 'Well, yes,' she said. 'I know I look awful. Enough to make you even sicker.' She laughed nervously.

'You look sensational,' he said fervently. 'Absolutely beautiful, the loveliest sight I've ever seen.'

She laughed again. She knew he was experiencing the euphoria that came after a sudden severe illness had passed.

'I'll bet you're hungry,' she said as she started towards the door.

'Starved,' he admitted. 'Ravenous.' He sat up and smiled at her, revealing strong even teeth, intensely white against his deep tan.

'I'll fix some breakfast,' she said. 'You might want to risk a bath and a shave if you feel strong enough. My father's gear is still in the bathroom. I've washed your clothes and put them on the dressing table, but I'll have to mend your shirt before you can wear it. I think you should stay in bed today anyway, and keep on with the penicillin.'

'I think you're right,' he said. Then, as she started to leave, he frowned. 'It's Laurie, isn't it?' he asked. She nodded. 'Laurie,' he repeated. He stared at her. 'I meant it, you know,' he said gravely. 'You are beautiful.'

She laughed lightly and ran her fingers through her hair again. 'Convalescents always feel that way about their nurses,' she said, and left the room.

# CHAPTER TWO

'TALK to me,' he said irritably.

It was later that afternoon. After a good breakfast he had slept most of the morning. Laurie had fixed him a bowl of soup for lunch, which he had eaten hungrily, asking for more. Now, feeling his strength returning, he was beginning to get restless.

'All right,' Laurie said quickly. She knew that once he was well he would want to leave, to go back to where he came from. She wanted to make him happy, to satisfy his whims, to keep him with her as long as possible. 'I'll finish mending your shirt.'

She sat down in the armchair by his bed and started sewing up the tears in the shirt. She could see that even in its disreputable condition, it was of good quality, possibly custom-made.

He was sitting up in bed leaning back on the pillows, his smooth chest and shoulders bare.

'Tell me about yourself,' he said.

Laurie shrugged. 'There really isn't very much to tell,' she replied. 'I was born and raised right here on Cadranelle.' She gave him a quick glance to see if he was amused by that admission, but he was watching her gravely, as if he was really interested. 'I know that must sound dull to you,' she said defensively.

'Not at all,' he replied. 'Not if you've been happy. That's all that counts. Have you?'

'Been happy?' she asked. She smiled. 'Oh, yes. I love the island. Yes, I've been very happy.' Then her face clouded over. 'That is, until . . .' She faltered and cleared her throat. 'You see, my father just died three months ago.' She concentrated hard on her sewing.

'And you still miss him,' he said softly.

She looked at him. 'Yes,' she said simply.

'How about your mother?'

'She died six years ago. She was a nurse.'

'Ah,' he said, 'I see how you came by your healing skills. In my limited experience with the medical profession, I've found that nurses do far more for their patients than doctors.' He paused. 'What will you do now?'

'I'm not sure,' Laurie replied. 'I'll be all right here for a while. I own the house outright and don't really need much money. I paint a little and have sold a few things to the tourists in the summertime. There are a lot of my father's unpaid bills on the books, so I'll be eating for some time anyway.'

'I'd like to see your work. Maybe I could help you. I know a few people in the art world.'

There was a short silence then. It dawned on Laurie that she knew absolutely nothing about this man.

'How about you?' she asked. 'I don't even know your name, where you're from, how you got here.'

'No,' he said slowly, 'you don't.' He frowned and turned his head away.

'I don't mean to pry,' Laurie said quickly. 'You don't need to tell me anything you don't want to.'

He turned back to her. 'My name is Miles Cutler.' He watched her carefully, as if to see her reaction, but the name meant nothing to her.

'That's a nice name,' she said. 'Unusual.' She continued sewing.

'My home is in Seattle,' he went on, 'but my business takes me all over the world, so I don't spend much time there. I came up to the islands alone on my boat, to get away for a while, cruise around the islands, do some fishing. I was out in the dinghy when I got caught in that storm, and ended up here in your house.'

Laurie wondered what his business was, but didn't like to ask. She held the shirt up in front of her, examining it.

'Well,' she said, 'it's somewhat the worse for wear, but at least it won't fall apart.'

She went over to the dresser, folded the shirt and put it on top of the trousers she had washed and ironed yesterday. She could sense his eyes following her as she moved about the room.

'How old are you, Laurie?' she heard him ask.

She turned around to face him. 'I'm twenty-one,' she replied.

He was gazing at her oddly, appraisingly, a strange gleam in the dark eyes.

'Why hasn't some local man snapped you up by now?' he asked.

His voice was easy, casual, but as their eyes met, Laurie was aware of a peculiar tension in the air.

She thought about Ted, comparing him to the man in the bed. One, she thought, was a very nice young boy, the other an obviously widely-experienced and fascinating man.

She sensed danger, but was not afraid. Two days ago she hadn't known Miles Cutler existed. She had taken him into her home, tended his wounds, nursed him. He could have been a criminal; he could be married with ten children. She didn't care. There was something in him that compelled her admiration, her trust—and yes, she admitted, a powerful physical attraction.

Laurie had never experienced a reaction like this to any man before in her life. She found it unsettling, but not at all frightening. She had a sudden overwhelming urge to run to the man in the bed, to put her hands on those broad shoulders, those powerful arms, that smooth chest.

'Well?' he said. 'Aren't you going to answer me?'

The spell was broken. Laurie laughed and gave her head a little shake. 'I don't know why,' she replied. 'I guess I'm just not interested. How about you? Do you have a family?' There, the question was out. It hung between them, until finally he shook his head slowly from side to side.

'No,' he said, 'I don't. I'm an orphan, too.'

'Well,' she said, 'I'd better start thinking about dinner. How does fresh salmon sound?'

'It sounds terrific!'

In the kitchen, at the far end of the long living room, Laurie absently started preparing their dinner. It would soon be dark. Already the sun had begun to set in the western sky.

Her thoughts were racing in wild confusion, distracting her from her cooking. She burned her hand when she put the potatoes into the oven to bake, and dropped cutlery when she set the table. When finally she cut her hand on the paring knife peeling carrots, she made herself stop short. She stood at the kitchen sink, her hands braced on the counter, staring out the window at the gathering dusk.

What in the world is happening to me? she wondered. Then she snorted softly to herself. Of course, even with her practically non-existent experience, she knew. She had read the forbidden books along with her friends in the school library. She had seen one or two racy movies on her rare trips into Victoria or Vancouver. She and Ted had exchanged a few mild, tentative kisses. After all, for heaven's sake, she was a doctor's daughter!

But the actual experience of desire was an entirely different thing. Perhaps, she thought, if she'd had more experience, the feelings that welled up in her now would not be so overpowering.

The sun set at last. It was growing dark outside. She sighed and picked up the paring knife again, resolving to be more careful. Then she noticed that her hand was still bleeding where she had cut it. She rinsed it off under the tap, then put her mouth to the wound, tasting the warm blood.

There was a sudden noise behind her, footsteps. She turned around. Miles was standing at the island counter, dressed now in his black trousers and patched white shirt, his eyes fastened on her bleeding hand.

'What have you done?' he asked.

'Oh, I was careless and cut my hand. It's nothing.'

He walked slowly towards her. As she watched him now, his strength back, moving about, he seemed so big, so tall, and much more disturbing now that he was no longer an invalid.

'Here,' he said, standing so close to her they were almost touching, 'let me see.'

Wordlessly, she held out her hand. He took it in his, and she watched, mesmerised, as the blood trickled slowly on to his own large hard.

'It's nothing,' she repeated.

'Do you have a band-aid?'

She nodded. 'Yes, in the cupboard, on the bottom shelf.'

He opened the cupboard door, took a Band-Aid out of the box sitting there and removed the protective plastic strips from the adhesive. Then, gently, carefully, he stuck it on her hand, holding it tight to stop the bleeding and secure the tape.

Still holding her hand, he looked down at her, smiling. 'There,' he said softly, 'now I've had a chance to nurse you.'

Laurie raised her clear grey eyes to meet his, and she felt as though she were drowning in those deep blue-green pools. There was a puzzled look on his face as he stared down at her, frowning slightly. Then, as she continued to hold his gaze in hers, a gleam appeared in those dark eyes.

She watched, hardly daring to breathe, as his head bent slowly down towards her. She closed her eyes, and without hesitation, with a sudden surge of joy, lifted her lips to meet his.

His kiss was gentle, but nothing at all like Ted's shy brotherly pecks. She sensed with certainty the passion behind the gentleness, and as his arms came around her, lightly clasping her to him, she sank against his chest with a sigh and reached up to put her hands on his shoulders.

Then, as her arms twined about his neck, his hold on her tightened, his mouth became harder, more insistent. His hands began to move up and down her back, sliding the thin material of her blouse over the bare skin beneath.

She opened her lips joyfully to receive him as his kiss deepened. Her whole body, pressing against his, was a flame.

Then, suddenly, he drew abruptly away from her, tore his lips from hers, and held her by the shoulders at arm's length.

'God, I'm sorry, Laurie,' he rasped harshly. 'I shouldn't have done that.'

Dismayed, Laurie lifted a hand and put it on his cheek. 'Why not, Miles?' she asked, bewildered.

He glared at her. 'Because you're only a child,' he barked. 'Because I should have known better. Because . . .' He broke off, his face hard and set. 'There are a lot of reasons,' he said grimly. 'You don't know anything about me.'

'I'm not a child,' Laurie retorted. 'I'm a responsible adult. I wanted to kiss you. I enjoyed it.

Don't I have any say?'

'Listen, Laurie, I'm thirty-five years old. I have a life you know nothing about. I . . .' He turned and stalked off away from her, stopping at the end of the counter.

Laurie stared at his back. His shoulders were slumped over. Of course, she thought, a powerfully attractive man like Miles Cutler would have his choice of beautiful, sophisticated women. Why should he be interested in a country doctor's daughter?

She realised, too, that he was still weak. She walked over to him and put a hand on his arm, and he flinched visibly under her touch.

'It's all right, Miles,' she said evenly, 'I understand. You've been ill, and I nursed you, so you're grateful. I read more into the kiss than you intended. I realise that compared to the women you must know, I'm only an ignorant country girl, but please, don't blame yourself.'

He whirled around then, fire in his eyes. He grabbed her by the shoulders. 'It's not that, damn it!' he shouted. 'You're not an ignorant country girl.' He put up a hand and stroked her silky black hair. 'You're a beautiful, fascinating, desirable young woman.'

She only stared at him gravely, not understanding. He smiled crookedly at her, then, and removed his hands.

'I'm going to leave tonight,' he said. He held up a hand at her look of dismay. 'I'm all right. I need to look after my boat. It's tied up at the public dock

and I want to see if it was damaged by the storm.'
He ran a hand through his crisp black hair. 'And
I've got to think.'

Laurie longed to ask him if she would ever see
him again, but a sixth sense told her to let him go,
that this was not a man to be pinned down against
his will, and he was obviously determined to go.

'Don't you want some dinner before you leave?'
she asked quietly.

He gazed down at her in frank and open
appreciation of her reaction. 'You're quite a girl,
Laurie,' he said. 'Far from an ignorant country girl,
and far from a child.' He smiled. 'Yes, I'd like
some dinner.'

After dinner, she walked downstairs with him
and up the path to the paved road that led down to
the public dock. He had brought nothing with him,
of course, and so had no belongings to collect and
carry.

Laurie had offered to take him over to the dock
in her little boat, securely moored under cover, but
he had refused.

'It's only a half-mile walk,' he said firmly. 'I need
the exercise.'

At the edge of the road, he turned to her. There
was a full moon again to light his way, and the road
was well marked. He bent down and kissed her
lightly on the cheek.

'Thanks again for everything, angel of mercy,' he
said. 'You probably saved my life.'

She looked up at him with a steady gaze. 'I don't
want your gratitude, Miles,' she said. 'I'm glad I

was there when you needed me. You probably should have that arm looked at by a doctor. Those stitches should come out in a few days.'

He nodded. 'Yes, doctor.' He put a hand lightly on her cheek. 'Goodbye, then, Laurie,' he said.

'Goodbye, Miles. Good luck.'

She watched him for a few moments as he walked off down the road. He seemed all right, she thought, strong enough by now for that short walk. He never looked back.

She turned, then, and with a heavy heart walked slowly back to the cottage. Briskly, methodically, she cleaned up the remains of their dinner and washed the dishes, trying hard not to think about Miles.

She pottered around until bedtime, trying to keep busy, hoping to tire herself by cleaning out the kitchen cupboards, doing a little mending.

Finally she undressed and got into bed, but sleep wouldn't come. She lay there, her mind in a turmoil, going over and over again the scene with Miles before dinner when he had kissed her.

Was it just gratitude? The euphoria of convalescence? Propinquity? He was obviously an experienced man. Why had he broken away from her when she had responded so ardently, willing, wanting to give herself to him wholly?

She wondered, too, why she felt no shame at her total response to him. Was it the stupidity of her inexperience, a juvenile naïveté that made her throw herself at the first strange man who showed an interest in her? Why had she been so willing to surrender to this man when Ted's timid advances only left her cold and aloof?

She sighed in bewilderment. She tossed and turned in the narrow bed, but her tormented mind would give her no rest. All she knew was that she wanted Miles Cutler, in any way, on any terms.

Finally, in despair, she got out of bed and began to prowl aimlessly about the house. When she came to the open door of the bedroom Miles had occupied, a strange force impelled her inside.

She looked down at the bed where he had lain. After his fever had broken, she had changed the bedclothes while he bathed. She knelt down on the bed, bent her head to his pillow, still indented from the pressure of his head. It seemed to her there was the lingering fragrance of his clean, masculine scent.

Then, slowly, the tears finally streaming from her eyes, she crawled under the covers and lay her head down on his pillow. At last she slept, as though enfolded once again in the strong arms of the man she longed for.

The next day dawned bright and clear. Laurie yawned and stretched, luxuriating in the bed Miles had occupied. With the advent of a new day and the release of tears the night before, the heavy load on Laurie's heart was lifted a little.

Besides, she thought to herself as she walked barefoot over to the window, he might come back to Cadranelle some day. I may see him again.

It was a beautiful day, Indian summer, the slight

breeze coming in through the open window mild and balmy. A good day for painting, she thought. She might even go for a swim. There was a small, clear lake about a quarter of a mile in towards the centre of the island, secluded and private now that the tourists had gone and the fishermen were all out on their boats. One could even safely swim there naked, but Laurie had never had the nerve to do so.

The thought of Miles still lay heavily on her mind, dampening her joy in the beautiful day, but even though she kept telling herself that she would probably never see him again, she didn't want to forget him. She wanted to remember how his arms had felt, holding her, and his lips pressed against hers, tenderly at first, then with growing desire.

In the afternoon, when the light was just right, she set up her painting things and took a good hard look at the portrait of her father and the blue of the sea that just wouldn't come right.

She wished now she had sketched Miles while he was here, but there had never seemed to be time. She looked again at the portrait, with Miles still on her mind, distracting her, and all of a sudden she knew how to get the colour of the sea right.

It was exactly the colour of Miles Cutler's eyes. Quickly she began mixing her paints, with a little less white in the blue, a little more green, until at last she had the colour she wanted, a beautiful deep greeny-blue, a dark aquamarine, a teal, that matched those eyes perfectly.

The rest was easy. She worked slowly, painstakingly. Now that she had the colour right, it was a simple matter to finish the background. As she worked, the thought formed in her mind that she could still do a sketch of Miles from memory, and she promised herself she would start work on it soon.

She was interrupted by the ringing of the telephone, and she ran inside to the old waiting room on the ground floor where the telephone was kept. As she answered it, she glanced at the clock. It was almost five. The afternoon had flown by.

It was Emma Bendiksen from the hotel on the line.

'Laurie,' came the familiar voice, 'how have you been? We haven't heard a word from you for days.'

'Oh, Emma,' Laurie replied, 'I'm all right. You shouldn't worry about me.'

'Who's worried?' said Emma huffily. 'I'm just getting sick of Carl's company and wondered if you'd come up to the hotel for supper tonight. With Ted and his dad and all the other fishermen gone up north, and the tourists out of my hair, I get lonely.'

Laurie smiled. Plump, gruff Emma Bendiksen did nothing but complain about the inconsiderate, demanding tourists when they descended on her every Memorial Day, and her vehemently-expressed diatribes against the local fishermen, their slovenly personal habits and their slowness to pay their bar and grocery bills had stung many an ear in the past.

'That sounds lovely,' she replied. She knew that one more evening alone so soon after Miles' departure would be a torment. 'What can I bring?'

'Just yourself, dearie,' was the curt reply. 'If I can get Debbie away from the television and her movie magazines long enough, maybe we can have a game of hearts or pinochle.'

The Bendiksens' hotel was on the one paved street the island boasted. The street, only a mile long, led from the public boat dock, up past the hotel, the small gift shop next door, and a hardware store across the street that specialised in all kinds of boating gear. From this minuscule 'business district', the road petered out past a few weather-beaten houses and became yet another deeply rutted path, baked hard in the summer, awash in the winter.

The hotel had accommodation for only ten guests. Most of the summer visitors came by boat and tied up at the public dock, renting rooms by the day mainly to take the long hot baths unavailable on their boats or to get away from their children for an afternoon of privacy.

The Bendiksens' main income was derived from the restaurant and tavern on the main floor. They had converted the old lobby into a cheerful room with a pub-like atmosphere. There were brightly-coloured Indian rugs on the floor, red and white checkered tablecloths on the six round tables, and pieces of oddly-shaped driftwood leaning against the pine-panelled walls.

Carl Bendiksen, an inveterate beachcomber, had collected several Japanese floats, those pale green glass bubbles that would occasionally wash up on the beach intact. He had displayed these prominently on the walls, and refused to part with them at any price.

Even though the evening was mild, Emma had built a roaring fire in the huge stone fireplace at one end of the room. There were candles in the jugs on all the tables against the swift and frequent power failures during the winter storms, but tonight the soft lamps were lit.

There were five at dinner, an odd quintet. Emma, as always, bustled about clucking and complaining, constantly on the move, while Carl sat silently puffing his pipe. He was a small, weather-beaten man who had spent most of his life fishing the Bering Sea until a shipwreck injury had left one arm paralysed and useless.

Their teenage daughter, Debbie, sullen and superior, had finally been persuaded and bullied to join them, and old Joe Folsom, who owned the hardware store, made the fifth.

Laurie was subdued and silent, even more quiet and reserved than usual. More than once she had caught Emma giving her a suspicious, questioning glance.

After dinner, they sat in comfortable chintz-covered chairs in front of the fire. Emma and Carl were arguing about whether to play hearts or pinochle.

'Five is too many for pinochle,' the laconic Carl stated flatly.

'That's nonsense. Any number can play pinochle. You just want to play hearts so you can cheat and shoot the moon.'

Carl, his old clay pipe clamped firmly between his teeth, only grunted, while Debbie sighed loudly, dramatically, in exasperation at her parents' bickering.

'I don't see why we have to play any game at all,' she announced sulkily. 'They're all so boring, just like everything else on this stupid island!'

Laurie had to smile at that. She and Debbie were only four years apart in age, but had never been friends. While Laurie loved the island and had always been content with her life there, the younger Debbie had longed to leave for as along as she could remember.

Laurie glanced at Emma, whose mouth had snapped open to deliver a stinging rebuttal to her daughter's sullen complaint. Laurie often wondered how the plump, untidy Emma and the morose, wizened Carl had managed to produce such a beautiful daughter.

Debbie Bendiksen was that rarity, a natural blonde, with long corn-silk hair flowing in soft natural waves down over her shoulders. She was small, with a perfect figure, a creamy complexion and huge violet eyes. Her beauty was only marred by her perennial expression of sullen rebellion.

'I'll tell you what,' old Joe Folsom piped up, 'let's have a round of darts.' He was the island champion and never missed an opportunity to display his skill.

There was a unanimous wave of protest from the others at that. No one wanted to challenge the undisputed master of the game. Joe retreated in a huff, muttering about poor sports and jealousy.

They finally, after more prolonged bickering, decided on hearts. Debbie consented ungraciously, saying that at least you didn't have to concentrate on such a childish game.

They gathered together about one of the round tables in front of the fire. While Joe dealt, Emma got up to get some beer. 'Will you help me, Laurie?' she asked, casting a disgusted look at the bored Debbie. 'Her Royal Highness is indisposed.'

Laurie rose quickly to her feet, hoping to forestall another argument. 'Of course, Emma,' she replied, just as Debbie opened her mouth in protest.

The two women went into the spotless kitchen, and Laurie watched as Emma got down glasses and put them on a tray.

'Just get the beer out of the fridge, would you, Laurie?' Emma asked.

Laurie did so and brought it over to the counter. 'Shall we pour it here?' she asked.

'No,' said Emma with a sigh. 'Carl says I never pour it right, that I bruise it, or some such nonsense.' As Laurie set the quart bottle down on the tray, she gradually became aware that Emma was staring at her. 'Are you okay, Laurie?' she asked at last.

Laurie turned to her. 'Of course. Why do you ask?'

She had a sudden, insane impulse to put her hand to her mouth, as if somehow Emma could sense Miles Cutler's kiss still burning there.

Emma had been the closest thing to a mother Laurie had known since her own mother died. She knew that any inquisitiveness on Emma's part was made out of love. But not for worlds would she have shared with anyone her experience of those two days with Miles.

'I just thought you were a little quieter than usual,' Emma replied brusquely. Then her voice softened. 'You still miss your father, don't you?'

Tears came to Laurie's eyes at the mention of her father. 'Yes,' she said, 'I do. But,' she added truthfully, 'it's getting better all the time.'

The game of hearts progressed without incident once it had been decided what the game would be. Debbie ostentatiously stifled an occasional yawn, and Emma shot Carl a baleful look when he did, indeed, shoot the moon, but he swept in his cards imperturbably, his pipe clenched firmly in his mouth.

At ten o'clock, Emma served coffee and wild huckleberry pie. They chatted amicably, desultorily before the dying fire, local gossip, humorous, condescending anecdotes about the tourists, how the fishermen would fare with their catch this year.

'Say,' Joe Folsom said in his high piping voice, 'I notice that fancy boat down at the public dock finally left.'

Laurie's ears perked up at that. He could only mean Miles' boat. She sat quietly, alert to the conversation as the others chimed in.

'You mean that fellow all by himself?' asked Carl. 'Out of the Seattle Yacht Club, according to the burgee. That was some boat. Custom-made Chris Craft—had to be sixty, seventy feet.'

'Well, I don't know anything about his boat,' Debbie chimed in, 'but I do know he was the most gorgeous man this backwater has ever seen!' She rolled her bright blue eyes in frank appreciation.

'Debbie!' Emma reprimanded, 'watch your tongue. A young girl like you! He was up here buying groceries last week, and he's years too old for you. And, I might add, more than a match for an inexperienced young girl.'

'Oh, Mother,' Debbie protested, 'what has age got to do with it?'

Carl chuckled. 'Don't worry, Emma. The likes of that particular man won't be bothering with our Debbie.'

'I heard he was some important business tycoon in the city,' Joe put in importantly. He was a stout man with fuzzy grey hair and a round pink baby face. His eyes were wide.

'Has to be rich to afford a boat like that,' commented Carl.

'Well,' Debbie said petulantly, 'I still say he's the greatest thing that ever hit this place.' She got up from her chair and flounced over to the door that led to the family's living quarters, then turned and faced her mother defiantly. 'And if he ever comes back, I for one have no intention of staying away from him!'

Emma started to rise from her chair, her mouth half open, a look of dismay on her plump face. 'Debbie . . .' she started to say, but the words died on her lips. Debbie was gone.

'Oh, leave her be, Em,' said Carl.

She turned on him. 'Leave her be!' She snorted and began to clear away the pie plates, muttering under her breath. 'Leave her be, indeed. That's all you know about it.' She paused and gave Laurie a stricken look. 'I don't know what I'm going to do about that girl, I honestly don't. She'll be the death of me!'

Laurie got up and went to her side. 'Oh, come on, Emma, she'll be all right. She just has to find her own way.'

Emma looked at her bleakly. 'Maybe. Maybe so.' She sighed deeply. 'Lord knows I've done all I can.'

The party broke up then. Laurie helped Emma put the dirty dishes in the dishwasher, then said goodnight and went off down the hill towards the cottage.

It was another bright moonlit night. After all the discussion of Miles this evening, Laurie felt restless. It was only ten-thirty. She knew she would never be able to sleep.

On an impulse, she decided to take a walk down to the boat dock before going home. Almost of their own volition, her feet had propelled her in that direction. The moon cast enough light so that she could make her way without using the flashlight she always carried, and even at night the shapes and terrain of the island were so familiar that the dark held no terrors for her.

As she walked slowly along the paved road that

rarely saw a vehicle of any kind, she thought over what the others had said about Miles.

Joe had said he was an important business tycoon, and Carl that he had to be rich to own a boat like that. Laurie laughed softly to herself. It didn't matter. She didn't see Miles as having any background, whether of wealth or poverty. During those few days he had spent with her, they were only a man and a woman, alone, isolated against any of the so-called realities of life in the world.

The boat dock was built at the bottom of the island crest, at sea level. As she started down the hill, Laurie could see by the moonlight its dark shape jutting out into the sheltered bay, hear the gentle lap of the surf splashing up against the sturdy pilings. Then a cloud passed in front of the moon.

An owl hooted. There was a rustling in the heavy underbrush on either side of the road. Laurie stopped some hundred yards away from the dock and peered down into the dimness.

There was no sign of a boat there. They had said it was gone, but she had still hoped it might still be there, that he had come back. With a heavy heart, she trudged slowly back up the road, then down the path to her house.

She was tempted that night to sleep in Miles' bed again, but her common sense told her she would have to put him out of her mind eventually, and she might as well start now.

As she undressed and got into her own bed, she couldn't help wondering if it had all been a dream. He had come with nothing and left without a trace

# CHAPTER THREE

THE next day, Laurie's determination to put Miles Cutler out of her mind as though he had never existed faltered as soon as she woke up with only thoughts of him on her mind.

The trouble was, she mused as she went into the bathroom to shower, he *did* exist. Nothing in her life had ever seemed as real to her as that one kiss. Still, she thought sensibly, brushing her teeth, there was another reality. He was gone, and she'd just have to face it.

She decided that what she needed to take her mind off him was some strenuous physical activity. It was another mild warm day, a good day to wash everything in sight and hang it out to dry.

After a hasty breakfast of orange juice, toast and coffee, she went into her bedroom, took off her robe and put on a pale blue cotton sundress and a pair of cotton briefs. Everything else she owned in her meagre wardrobe would get washed. It was time to get her heavier clothes ready for winter, anyway.

She gathered together every washable piece of wearing apparel and took it downstairs to the small laundry room at the back of the ground floor. While that load was washing, she went back upstairs and stripped her bed.

49

Then, steeling herself, she went into her father's old bedroom. It seemed to her as she went in that if she tried hard she could still picture Miles lying in the bed, the dark tousled head against the pillow, the deep eyes watching her as she moved about the room, the strong tanned shoulders and arms lying outside the covers.

No, she said firmly to herself, I will not do that. She gritted her teeth and marched over to the bed. She would wash everything, she decided, blankets and all, get every last trace of him out of the house.

As she leaned down to pick up the bedding she had placed on the floor, her eye was caught by a flash of white under the bed. She got down on her hands and knees and reached out to retrieve it.

It was a towel, the same one, she realised, that she had fastened around Miles' waist that first night so that she could take off his wet trousers. She held it in her hands, staring down at it, remembering how he had looked standing there so pale and shaken, yet so strong and compelling.

A great sob rose in her throat, shaking her whole body, and finally the tears came. She buried her face in the towel and let loose the torrent she had bottled up inside in her effort to be strong and sensible.

When the frenzy finally passed, she felt better. She bathed her swollen face and combed her hair and with renewed resolution carried the bedding downstairs.

\*    \*    \*

By three o'clock, the wash was all hung out on the line, and Laurie had even been able to take in some of the lighter pieces. The warm sun and slight breeze had dried much of it by then.

After lunch she set up her easel out in the clearing and got to work finishing the background of her father's portrait. Now that she had the colour of the sea right, she was anxious to start on a new seascape. The summer tourists seemed to like those best, perhaps as a memento of the island, a reminder of the beauty and majesty of the unfathomable sea.

She had finished the portrait and taken in the rest of the washing by five o'clock. The sun was lowering now in the western sky. Once it went down, dusk would fall quickly, and it would grow too cool for the brief blue sundress.

Laurie sat down on one of the garden chairs and leaned back to survey the portrait. She was satisfied with it at last. Idly, she put her head back and closed her eyes, listening to the familiar island sounds, the screeching of the gulls, the lap of the surf on the rocks below, the rustling of the giant cedars.

As she let go, feeling peaceful and pleasantly tired from her day's labours, she drifted into a light sleep.

A sudden strange sound, a crackling in the underbrush, disturbed her reverie. It wasn't unusual for deer to come this close to the cottage after the hubbub created by the summer tourists was over.

Slowly she opened her eyes. There before her, not ten feet away at the edge of the clearing, stood Miles Cutler. Laurie blinked. Was she dreaming? She sat up straighter, and a little cry escaped her lips.

He was standing by a tall birch tree, his hand resting on the slim white trunk. He had on a greyish-green knit shirt and darker grey cotton trousers. He looked tall and tan and strong, and he was smiling at her.

'Miles,' she whispered. She stood up. She wanted to run to him, to throw herself into his arms, to feel his heart beating next to hers, his lips on her mouth. But she felt suddenly shy, rooted to the spot. She put a hand to her breast. 'You've come back.'

Slowly he started walking towards her until he stood before her. He looked down at her.

'Yes,' he said quietly, 'I've come back.' He ran a hand through his thick dark hair. 'I had to see you again.' He smiled crookedly, crinkling up the little lines at the corners of his eyes. 'I wanted to make sure you weren't just a figment of my feverish imagination.'

She smiled shyly. 'How did you get here? Did you walk?'

'No. When I left here I ran the boat down to Friday Harbor and picked up a new dinghy. I rowed over from the dock—no storm today. I can't stay. I just wanted to see you again, to thank you.'

Her heart sank. What did that mean? Since he had left, two days ago, she had built up such a fantastic vision in her mind of what their reunion would be like if they ever saw each other again that the reality deflated her.

She had imagined they would rush blindly, passionately into each other's arms. Yet now here they stood, like two strangers. She hardly knew what to say to him.

She looked at his arm. There was a fresh dressing on it.

'How is your arm?' she asked stiffly. 'It looks as though you've had it properly attended to.'

'Yes. I stopped in at Dr Finney's in Friday Harbor. It's fine. He took the stitches out—said you'd done a fine job. He spoke very highly of your father—and of you.'

He was gazing at her with a strange unsmiling intensity, but still he made no move, no gesture that would indicate that their relationship had ever been more than nurse and patient.

He's only being polite, she thought to herself in an agony of self-condemnation. Here I had built up one kiss in my mind to enormous proportions, and all it was on his part was gratitude.

'Well,' she said at last, 'I'm glad to hear you're all right. It was kind of you to stop by.'

His gaze faltered then. He glanced down at the portrait of her father, then turned and gave it a closer inspection.

'That's quite good, you know,' he said, and turned to her. 'You're very like your father. The same wonderful colouring—the clear grey eyes and black hair.' He laughed. 'It's amazing how tolerably good looks in a man can become incandescent beauty in a woman.'

Laurie didn't know what to reply to that. What did he mean? Laurie knew she was attractive—Ted had told her so often enough, and she'd had to beat off her share of errant husbands and lecherous schoolboys among the summer tourists.

She knew that her black hair shone, that her eyes were clear, her pale skin smooth. She led a healthy life and took care of herself. She knew, too, that her features were regular, her body slim and firm. What she didn't realise was how striking the totality of her looks became. Her face and figure were undeniably attractive, but her air of reserve, of quiet dignity, her inner beauty, had a strong impact on masculine eyes jaded by aggressive, overtly seductive and sophisticated women that she didn't dream of.

She could only stare down at her bare feet, tongue-tied. She felt stupid and awkward, uncomfortable in the childish blue sundress with, she suddenly realised, hardly another stitch on underneath it. Would Miles think she was being deliberately seductive?

'Well,' said Miles, breaking the long silence, 'I'd better be off before it gets dark. I have to be in Seattle for a meeting the day after tomorrow, and I'll be alone on the boat going down. Then I have to go away, out of the country, on business.'

He turned to go, and panic rose in Laurie's throat. Suddenly she knew she couldn't let him go like this. If there was the smallest chance that his feelings for her even remotely approached what she felt for him, she had to gamble on that chance. She knew she might be making a terrible mistake, but she didn't care. Every fibre of her being ached for his presence. She lifted her head.

'Miles,' she said, 'wouldn't you like something to eat before you go?'

He cocked his head to one side. 'Still playing nurse?' he asked.

She shook her head slowly from side to side. 'No,' she said simply. 'I just don't want you to go just yet.'

Because I may never see you again, she added to herself. Because I must find out if you really have no feeling for me but gratitude.

He seemed to be debating within himself. He stood quite still. The sun was setting now, and soon it would be dark. He glanced up at the sky, where a pale moon had already appeared. Then he looked at Laurie and smiled.

'All right,' he said. 'The moon should be light enough to get me back to the dock later. There shouldn't be any other boats in my way, and it's not far.'

While Miles went down to the beach to tie up his dinghy more securely, Laurie went upstairs to prepare a light supper. There was fresh crab and the last of the greens and tomatoes from the garden for a large salad. She took some rolls she had baked last week out of the freezer and for dessert there were wild blackberries and cream.

Her heart sang as she set the table for two. Miles

is here, Miles is here. Soon she heard his step on the stair, his voice calling to her.

'Shall I bring in your painting things?'

'Oh, please,' she called back. She had forgotten all about them in her wild elation.

By the time he came upstairs it was dark outside. She had finished the salad and was putting the rolls in the oven to warm when he popped his head in the door.

'I'll just go and wash,' he said.

Laurie lit the candles on the table. It looked very pretty, she thought, surveying the gold chrysanthemums in a pottery bowl, the fresh white napkins and gleaming silver. She frowned. She wished she had some wine. Not a drinker herself, she never thought to buy any liquor. Then she remembered the brandy downstairs in her father's surgery. Maybe they could have a glass after dinner.

While they ate, Laurie felt her tension ebbing away. Fixing dinner for Miles had given her something to do, to occupy her mind. Now it seemed perfectly natural to have him sitting opposite her, obviously enjoying the food she had prepared for him.

'This trip you're taking,' she said. 'Where are you going? Or is it a secret?'

'No,' he replied. 'No secret. That is, where and why aren't, but the details are.' He leaned back in his chair and lit a cigarette. 'That was a wonderful dinner, Laurie. Is there no end to your talents.

She laughed. 'Would you like some brandy?

There's still almost a full bottle down in the surgery.'

'I remember,' he said with a grim look. 'I'll go down and get it.'

While he was gone, Laurie cleared the table and got out the glasses. She set them on the coffee table in front of the fireplace and lit the fire. The evenings were growing chilly and she still had on only the thin sundress.

When Miles came back, he sat down beside her on the couch in front of the fire and poured the brandy into the glasses.

'Tell me about your trip, Miles,' said Laurie. The brandy and the fire had warmed her, and she felt relaxed and happy. 'That is, as much as you can.'

He was leaning back on the couch, his long legs stretched out in front of him. Laurie thought she could never get enough of just looking at him. He was like a god to her, and she gazed intently at him, wanting to memorise every detail, knowing that this might be the last time she would ever see him.

'My family is involved in banking,' he told her. 'Metro.' He saw the blank look on her face. 'The Metropolitan Bank of the North-west,' he explained. 'My grandfather founded the bank, and my father expanded it considerably before he died. Went public on the stock exchange.'

'That sounds impressive,' she remarked.

'Not really,' he said. 'It's still a small bank, but we like it that way. We give excellent service to a small number of customers who trust us.'

'And what is your job?'

'I'm sort of a troubleshooter,' he said, grinning. 'They don't trust me with the important details, but I do have a knack for negotiating loans with foreign corporations who know our reputation for discretion and honesty.'

'Where do you go on your trips?'

'All over the world, anywhere I'm needed. This time I'm going to the Middle East.'

'It sounds fascinating,' said Laurie. 'I've never been anywhere.'

'Oh, you soon get tired of travelling,' he said. There was a wistful note in his voice. 'There's a lot to be said for having a permanent home.'

'Yet, you never married.'

He gave her an odd look. 'No,' he said gravely. 'I never had the time. Or never met the right person. I'll probably settle down one of these days. Perhaps before I'm forty. I'd like a family before I'm too old.'

They chatted companionably for some time, about his work, about Laurie's life on the island. Miles was especially entertained by her stories of the summer tourists, commenting that it was edifying and instructive to hear about them for a native's point of view.

Finally, as the fire began to die out, he rose to his feet and set his glass down on the table. He stood gazing down at her.

'It's time I left, Laurie,' he said quietly. 'I want to get an early start in the morning.'

'Yes, of course,' she said, jumping to her feet.

'I'll walk down to the beach with you.'

'No,' he said abruptly, a harsh note in his voice. 'No,' he repeated more gently. 'I'll say goodbye here, and thank you again for everything.'

In spite of her best intentions to be strong and brave, Laurie felt the tears sting her eyes, and was grateful for the dimness of the room in the flickering firelight, hoping he wouldn't notice.

She turned her head away from him. 'I don't want your thanks, Miles,' she said, and was dismayed at the way her voice cracked and faltered.

'Hey,' he said, 'what's wrong?' He crossed the few feet that separated them and put a hand under her chin, forcing her to look up at him. 'What's this? Tears?'

'No, no,' she said hastily, forcing a smile. 'Of course not.'

'Laurie,' he said gravely, 'the last thing I want, the last thing I intended, was to harm you in any way. That's why . . .' His voice broke off and he looked away.

'That's why what, Miles?' she asked gently.

She gazed up at his profile. His handsome features seemed tortured, as if he were undergoing some inner struggle. Slowly he turned back to her. His face was drawn and haggard.

'Why I'm leaving,' he ground out. 'Why I should never have come back.'

She held his gaze in hers steadily, by sheer power of will. 'But I'm glad you came back, Miles,' she said firmly. 'I wanted you to come back. If you hadn't, *that* would have hurt me.'

'Oh, God,' he breathed. 'Laurie, Laurie, what have I done?'

With a groan he put his arms around her and pulled her close against him, burying his face in her silky hair, holding her tightly, like a drowning man clinging to a life raft.

A searing flame of bliss coursed through Laurie's whole being. Eagerly she raised her hands and put them on his face, drawing them over the high prominent cheekbones, the rough flat planes of his jaw, his lips.

'I love you, Miles,' she whispered.

What a joy it was to be able to utter those words at last! She laughed gaily, deep in her throat. 'I love you.'

Then his mouth was on hers, sensuous, demanding, probing. Her lips parted joyfully to receive him as she arched her body closer, closer to him.

His hands were moving feverishly over her back, her bare shoulders and arms, then down to her hips, pulling her against him so that she could feel his hard masculine need.

His mouth left hers. She sighed and let her head fall backwards as his mouth descended to her throat and one hand came around to firmly clasp her breast. At that touch, the first she had ever experienced, Laurie's head fell back even farther as the most exquisite sensation of sheer physical pleasure pierced her whole body.

Then, roughly, he pushed down the shoulder straps of her sundress, and she heard him gasp as her nakedness was revealed to him. His hands and his mouth worshipped the full young breasts, and the dress slipped slowly to the floor.

He lifted her up in his arms and carried her into her bedroom. When he reached the side of the bed, he called her name.

'Laurie.' His voice was husky. She opened her eyes and gazed up into his. 'Do you want this?' he asked.

For answer, she reached her hands up to cup his face, then slid them down over his shoulders, his chest, and slowly began to unbutton his shirt.

He drew in his breath sharply. In the dim room, illuminated only by the light from the hall and the moon streaming in through the window, he watched her hands do their work.

Then he laid her down on the bed. Quickly he slipped off the shirt, the grey trousers. Laurie watched, transfixed by the sight of that masculine form, the strong broad shoulders and smooth muscled chest, the narrow hips and long powerful legs.

When he lay down beside her, their naked bodies touching for the first time, Laurie threw her arms around him, almost fainting with joy as his hands travelled up and down her firm young body, feverish now in his own obvious longing.

Then she felt a piercing stab of pain. She cried out once, then clutched at him tightly, holding him to her, as she felt him rise up as if to withdraw from her.

'No, Miles, no,' she whispered. 'It's all right— please!'

It was then that the exquisite sensations began, building up to an explosion, an earthquake, that sent tremors, shock waves of pleasure through her whole body.

Afterwards, as they lay side by side in the dimness, Miles rose up on one elbow and, leaning over her, began to stroke her hair back from her forehead.

'God, Laurie,' he muttered brokenly, 'I had no idea. Why didn't you tell me it was the first time for you?'

She put her fingers on his lips and smiled up at him. 'What would you have done if I had?' she asked.

He frowned. 'I would have left.'

'That's why I didn't tell you,' she said simply. 'I wanted this more than I've ever wanted anything.'

He let his head fall back on the pillow and raised an arm up to cover his eyes. 'You don't understand,' he said with a groan. 'I really do have to leave Cadranelle in the morning.'

'Don't worry,' she said, her hand on his mouth. 'I know you have to go. I know I may never see you again—our lives are so different. But we have tonight. You'll stay here until morning?'

He moved his arm from his eyes and touched her lightly on the lips, a crooked smile on his face.

'Yes,' he said, 'I'll stay.'

They slept then. Towards morning, at the first meagre light, Laurie awakened with her head on Miles' shoulder, his arm lying lightly across her waist.

Her heart was full of an almost transcendent joy as she watched the steady breathing and fine features of the man sleeping quietly at her side. His dark hair was tousled, falling over his forehead. She could see the shadow on his flat cheeks, the slight bristle of his beard. She gazed at the hollow of his long throat, the little pulse beating there, drank in his clean masculine fragrance.

She wanted to memorise every detail to carry with her always, and longed to run her fingers over the sensuous mouth, the firm chin, the muscled shoulders and arms.

Suddenly he stirred, as if aware of her gaze. He opened his eyes, blinked, and opened them again, and once again she was struck by the deep blue-green colour, the colour of the sea.

He smiled at her and reached up a hand to her cheek.

'Good morning,' he said. His hand went to the back of her head, and he pulled her down to kiss her lightly on the mouth.

Then his eyes closed again. Laurie decided to let him sleep; he had a long day ahead of him all alone in the boat. She put her head back on the pillow and shut her eyes, simply basking in the feel of his body next to hers. Gently she began to drift off to sleep again on a wave of contentment.

She was awakened by the delicious sensation of his hand moving on her breast, the fingers gently teasing the nipples which began hardening into points as fire raged through her. She smiled and stretched like a contented cat as his hands moved slowly, lightly, tantalisingly over her body. She felt his mouth on her lips, light, feathery, then under her ear, her throat, until finally it came to rest on her breast.

She arched her body towards him eagerly, and his arms came hard around her, gathering her to him, his mouth on hers, thrusting, insistent, demanding.

This time there was no pain, only a glorious sensation of sheer pleasure almost painful in its intensity, then an explosion that raised a cry of joy to her lips, then a deep, satisfying release.

Miles lay for a long time with his head on her breast while she ran her hands idly through his dark hair, crisp and thick in her fingers, and down over the nape of his neck. Soon the sun began to stream through the window, and he raised his head and looked down at her.

He put a hand on her cheek. 'God, you're so beautiful,' he said with a groan. 'How can I leave you?'

Laurie's heart soared. Maybe he would stay. She hardly dared breathe. She waited, watching him, as he looked blankly out the window, frowning, deep in thought.

'I've got to go,' he said flatly.

'Yes,' she whispered, 'I know.'

Miles got out of bed, then, and put on his trousers. She sat up, watching him, pulling the sheet up to cover herself, suddenly shy now that he was leaving. He buckled his belt, slipped on his shirt, and sat down on the edge of the bed to put on his socks and shoes.

'I'll fix you some breakfast,' she said.

'No, I'm not hungry. There's plenty on the boat.' He grinned. 'If I stayed for breakfast I might never leave!'

Laurie lowered her eyes. She longed to ask him if she would ever see him again, but a sixth sense told her that this was a man who couldn't be pushed or pinned down. He had promised her nothing. He hadn't taken her, she had given herself to him.

'I understand,' she said, forcing a smile.

'Yes,' he said gravely, 'and I'm counting on that understanding heart of yours. But there's a lot you don't understand. I have a lot of—' he hesitated '—unfinished business to take care of. But I promise you this, Laurie, I will come back.'

'That's all I want,' she whispered.

He kissed her lightly on the mouth and was gone. She slipped on her black robe and ran to the window to watch him striding down the path that led to the beach.

He turned once, saw her at the window and raised a hand. She returned the salute, then he rounded the bend past the clump of birches and was out of sight.

A line from a poem she had read once came to her mind: 'I could not love thee, dear, so much, Lov'd I not honour more.' Miles was going where his duty called him. She loved him for that. It was part of his integrity, his character, she knew, that he could give up what he wanted to fulfil his responsibilities.

Yet, she thought, as she walked slowly to the bathroom to take a shower, he hadn't uttered one word of love. She glanced at the rumpled bed as she walked by, and the colour rushed to her cheeks.

How wanton she had been with him! Did he think it was her nature to fall into bed with every attractive man who came her way? Yet how could he? He knew it was the first time for her, that she had given herself to him freely out of love.

She showered and dressed, then had a light breakfast. She took a cup of coffee outside and sat in the sun out in the little clearing at the back of the house, and sat there for a long time pondering his last words.

'I promise you this, Laurie,' he had said, 'I will come back.'

Wasn't that a commitment of sorts? He had said there were things she didn't understand about his life. Maybe he was married. No, she thought, he had said he wasn't, and Miles wouldn't lie to her.

She felt lethargic out there in the warm sunshine, without energy, as though her muscles had turned to jelly, her bones to dust. The night of passionate lovemaking and Miles' leaving so abruptly had left her drained, without the will to act.

Later that afternoon she walked down to the boat dock. He was gone, as she knew he would be, and she pictured him alone on his boat, the long trip down to Seattle through the inland waters. At least the weather was fine. He shouldn't have any trouble, but it was a tiring trip for a man to make alone.

As she turned to retrace her steps back to her house, she wondered for the hundredth time if she would ever see him again. He said he would come back, she reminded herself firmly. I must hang on to that promise.

# CHAPTER FOUR

OCTOBER passed into November. The leaves were gone from the trees now, and the landscape was stark and forbidding. Laurie kept busy. She had already finished two seascapes to sell next summer, and had made several sketches of Miles from memory.

When he comes back, she would tell herself, I'll do a coloured portrait so that I can paint those eyes, the colour of the sea.

She kept looking for some word from him, but as the weeks passed and no letter came, no phone call, she began to lose hope. She reminded herself over and over again that he would write or call if he could. From the newspaper accounts, there was new fighting in the Middle East, and she told herself that the mail was probably affected.

He could have been killed by terrorists, she thought, and I'd never know. Still, a little part of her would not give up hope. He promised he would come back, she would tell herself, and he will.

Towards the end of November, a group of trial lawyers from Seattle looking for an isolated spot to hold a small convention descended on Cadranelle. The hotel was jammed and Emma frantic. Laurie helped her during the week the lawyers were there, working long hours to get them fed and their rooms cleaned. Even Debbie pitched in.

The distraction was good for Laurie and helped to pass the time. When it was over, however, she had to face a fact that had been looming in her mind for weeks.

She had suspected for some time that she might be pregnant, and by the first of December, she was quite sure. By now her hopes that Miles would return, or at least get some word to her, had faded.

Sometimes their brief time together seemed like a dream. At others, she could recall him so vividly, his smile, the way he looked at her, the dark hair, the strong body next to hers, and then it seemed she could almost reach out and touch him.

Finally, one dreary rainy day in early December, she sat in front of the fire staring into the flickering flames, and knew she would have to come to a decision about her future. Either Miles had forgotten her or was unable to contact her. In either case, she was going to have a baby, and it looked as though she would have to do it alone.

But what to do? She rejected the idea of an abortion the second it popped into her mind. As a doctor's daughter, she could never condone the taking of a life. Even an unborn baby was, to her, a real human being, a person with rights of its own.

It was settled, then, that she would have the baby. She considered adoption next, but rejected that immediately, too. No matter what had happened to Miles, she had loved him, still loved him, and she couldn't give up his child.

She couldn't bear to have her old friends on Cadranelle know of her predicament. Emma and Carl, Joe Folsom, Debbie. And Ted! What would they think? Quiet, reserved Laurie Cochran, pregnant by an unknown man. She could never face that.

She would have to go away, she decided. But where? She would need to see a doctor soon. She was young and strong and healthy, but she knew from experience that anything could go wrong. She didn't want to go to Dr Finney in Friday Harbor; he had thought so highly of her father and of her.

She got up and began to pace the room. She wanted to get far away from Cadranelle. She'd need a job of some kind. A city—that was it.

She'd go to Seattle, she decided, and a part of her knew that it drew her because Miles lived there. An instinct she didn't understand seemed to impel her to the place where the father of her child was.

She would make no attempt to see him, she decided. He had forgotten about her by now. But still she wanted to be near him.

Her decision made, the next morning after breakfast Laurie walked up to the hotel to visit Emma Bendiksen. It was cold and damp out, with a heavy leaden sky overhead. She put on her boots and loden jacket and tied a scarf over her head.

Emma was in the kitchen baking bread.

'It smells heavenly in here, Emma,' Laurie remarked as she entered the familiar big kitchen.

Emma turned around. Her plump face, red from

her exertions and the heat of the oven, became wreathed in a broad smile when she saw Laurie.

'Laurie!' she cried. 'Come in. Take off your things and sit down. I've got a fresh pot of coffee on.'

Over coffee, Laurie told Emma of her plans to leave Cadranelle. The older woman was stricken, and tears appeared in the faded blue eyes.

'Oh, my dear, what will I do without you? You've been like my own child since your mother died. And what will become of you? How will you live?'

She pleaded with Laurie to change her mind, at least to think it over for a while longer, but Laurie was firm.

'No, Emma, I've made up my mind. I've got to try it. I love Cadranelle, but it's time I saw what the rest of the world was like.'

Emma only sighed and wiped her eyes. 'I expected this from Debbie,' she said reproachfully, 'but never from you, Laurie.'

Laurie smiled. 'Oh, Em, it's not the end of the world, and it's probably not for ever. I'll be back.'

In the end it was Emma who checked ferry and bus schedules and made the arrangements for Carl to take Laurie across the straits to Sidney on Vancouver Island where she could get the ferry to the mainland. Although Carl's left arm was useless, handling a boat was second nature to him.

They watched the weather reports carefully and chose a day that was cold and calm for the hour-long trip. Laurie only packed two suitcases, just taking the essentials. There was enough money, she had figured out, to keep her for a month and to buy whatever clothes she would need.

Emma had promised to look after the house for her. If she didn't come back, she could rent it out for the summer next year. It was too soon to face the possibility of selling it.

As she walked through the house on that last morning, it was all she could do to stick to her resolution. This was her home. She had grown up here, been happy here. And, she thought with a pang as she shut the door to her father's bedroom, loved Miles Cutler here.

But that seemed a hundred years ago, almost a dream. She squared her shoulders and marched down the hall to her own room to collect her suitcases. The decision was made; she would stick to it.

They all came down to the dock to see her off, Emma fighting back tears, Debbie wild with envy, Joe Folsom goggle-eyed with curiosity.

'I don't see why it should be you leaving instead of me!' Debbie hurled at her as a parting shot, her beautiful face sullen and resentful. Then she brightened and ran up to Laurie as she was stowing her suitcases on the deck. She grabbed her arm. 'Listen, Laurie, maybe when you get settled, find a job, a place to live, I can come down and stay with you.'

Laurie smiled wanly, thinking of the baby and how attractive *that* fact would be to Debbie's romantic expectations. She had no intention of communicating with her friends on the island in any case, at least until after the baby was born.

'I'll let you know, Debbie,' she said, and gave the hand a squeeze. She turned to Emma. 'Well, Em, thanks for everything. Don't worry about me—I'll be all right.'

Emma, weeping openly, threw her plump arms around the girl and held her tight. Then she released her and turned her head away, unable to speak.

'Goodbye, Joe,' Laurie called as she jumped up into the boat. 'Take care!'

Carl had the engines all warmed up, and after Laurie had untied the ropes from the cleats along the dock and pulled in the heavy canvas fenders, he nosed the boat towards the channel that led from the sheltered bay to the open straits.

The little group stood waving until the boat rounded the bend and disappeared. Laurie choked down a sob as she saw her friends vanish from sight. Then she turned into the wind, facing forward, her jaw set with determination.

In the calm sea they made good time across the straits. Carl, blessedly silent, his pipe clamped between his teeth, manoeuvred the boat skilfully with his one good arm. Except for a lonely school of porpoises and the ever-present seagulls, they had the sea to themselves.

Sidney was a busy harbour, a main port for ferries and freighters passing to and from Puget Sound on the inland waterway. Since they were an American boat in Canadian waters, they had to go through the Customs procedure, but it didn't take long at this time of year. A serious, courteous young officer came aboard, asking a few questions as to cargo and destination, and signed the entry sheet.

All the while, although his manner was stiff and formal, Laurie could feel his eyes on her as he looked through the boat and talked to Joe.

'You're not bringing anything into Canada, then?'

'Nope,' Carl replied tersely. 'Just the girl here.'

The officer's eyes lit on her again, then dropped to the form he was filling out.

'May I see your registration?'

Joe had it ready, familiar with the drill, and handed it to him wordlessly. The officer glanced at it briefly and gave it back.

'Righto, then,' he said. 'Everything seems to be in order. Thank you, Mr Bendiksen.' He tipped his cap to Laurie, then, and smiled for the first time. 'If you're going up to the ferry terminal, miss,' he said, 'I'm headed that way myself. You look like you could use some help with those bags.'

Laurie smiled back at him. 'Oh, I'm stronger than I look.' His face fell. 'But I'd be glad of your help,' she added quickly.

She turned to say goodbye to Joe, who astounded her by touching her cheek lightly with his forefinger, the only gesture of overt affection she had ever seen him make.

'Take care, then, Laurie,' he muttered gruffly. 'And call us if you need anything.'

Laurie gave him a brief hug and smiled at him through the tears that had come at this unexpected display of gentleness. She turned to the officer, who had already stowed her suitcases on the dock. He held out a hand to help her, and she forbore to tell him she had been jumping in and out of boats by herself since she was old enough to walk.

'You live on Cadranelle, then, do you, miss?' he asked as they trudged up the wooden steps to the ferry terminal.

Laurie hesitated. 'I did. I'm moving to Seattle.'

He looked at her with disappointment. 'Then you won't be coming back to Sidney?'

Laurie looked at him—really looked at him—for the first time. His hair was sandy, cut short under the peaked cap. He was young, about Ted's age, with a frank, open countenance. Not handsome, but with a pleasant smile.

She looked at his identification badge: Officer John Donaldson. A Scot. The thought flashed through her mind that under different circumstances, this was the kind of man she should want. Or Ted. Kind, unassuming men, unexciting, but steady and reliable.

He was obviously interested in her. What demon kept her from responding to men like this? A demon she never knew resided in her breast before she had met Miles Cutler. It was a force she could no more control than the beating of her own heart.

'No,' she said at last, 'I won't be coming back.' Not with a baby to care for, she added to herself.

'Well then,' he said, setting her bags down, 'here

we are.' He tipped his cap to her again, his face a polite mask. 'Have a pleasant trip, miss.'

'Thank you,' she murmured. 'Thank you for your help, Officer Donaldson. You've been very kind.' She watched him as he walked off.

He had deposited her bags at the ticket counter. She bought a ticket to Anacortes, on the Washington coast. From there she would take a bus into Seattle. After that, she didn't know what she would do.

It was early evening by the time the bus pulled into the depot in Seattle. Laurie had been to the city only once, several years ago, when they had brought her mother down to the famous Virginia Mason Clinic. It was there that the cancer they had suspected and that finally killed her had been diagnosed.

She remembered that she and her father had stayed in a small inexpensive apartment hotel for the few days they had been in town, the Barclay. It was located at the top of Pill Hill, the name given to it by Seattleites because it housed most of the city's clinics and hospitals.

Laurie's vague hope was that she could get work at one of them. She had no formal training, but a wide and varied experience of nursing.

She took a taxi to the Barclay. As they drove through the city streets, she gazed out of the window with awed eyes at the tall buildings, the throngs of people crowding the streets, the heavy traffic, the brightly-lit shops.

Her heart sank, and she felt a little faint. How in the world would she ever find her way in this maze of confusion and noise? As the taxi started up the steep hill on Madison Street and over the freeway with its steady stream of vehicles rushing by, Laurie looked out the back window at the busy harbour behind her.

Puget Sound, she thought with relief—a landmark at last. Now at least she had a sense of direction.

She noticed several electric trolleys going up and down the busy street. She would have to learn her way around on them. Taxis were too expensive.

The taxi deposited her in front of the familiar hotel, a small four-storey building with a restaurant on the main floor. Laurie paid the driver and stood on the sidewalk with her two suitcases.

The excited pounding of her heart, she realised, had turned from fear and confusion to a sense of exhilaration. Miles is here in this city, she thought to herself. I may never see him, but we are at least breathing the same air.

With renewed courage and a sense of adventure, she walked inside the hotel.

The apartment was tiny, clean, but drab and impersonal. There was one window, with a view of the brick wall of a neighbouring building. A threadbare carpet of nondescript colour, a couch that made into a bed and an easy chair that didn't match, a television set, a table and lamp, and that was about it.

Laurie's heart sank. It was a far cry from her home on Cadranelle with its comfortable furniture, light airy rooms and view of the sea. There was a tiny kitchen and bathroom, no more than large closets.

Lying in bed that night, listening to the unfamiliar sounds of the city, Laurie tossed and turned in the strange bed. A siren wailed in the distance and a plane went by overhead. From the street below, she could hear the endless cars go by, muted shouts, music from the restaurant.

She thought about Miles. He had promised he would come back, and he hadn't. Why? She couldn't believe he had just used her. She remembered the look of dismay on his face when he discovered he was the first man to make love to her.

And now, she thought, I'm carrying his child. What can I do? As she lay, miserable, in the darkness, suddenly there flashed into her mind some words of her father's after her mother died and Laurie was prostrate with grief.

'Laurie,' he had said severely after one of her fits of uncontrolled weeping, 'there are three enemies to peace of mind—guilt, self-pity and bitterness. Whenever they come to you, nip them in the bud. Don't let them get a foothold in your mind. Face the facts, assess your situation, then accept the worst that can happen. Then you'll discover your real options.'

All right, Dad, she said to herself, I'll try. With an effort of will she calmed herself so she could think. I'm pregnant and alone. My money will run out in a month. But I can work. I have friends, a home if I choose to go back to it. I have my health.

Then she smiled to herself and placed her hands on her still-flat abdomen. And I'm going to have Miles Cutler's baby, she thought. For the first time the growing life inside her became a reality, and she knew with a fierce surge of joy that no matter what happened, she would love this baby, that she would have a part at least of the man she still loved.

During the next two weeks, Laurie's resolution flagged as she made the rounds of the nearby hospitals and clinics looking for work. She had made out a list of likely places and conscientiously trudged to each new place, her spirits drooping with each polite rejection.

By now, she was almost ready to call it quits, to get on the next bus back to Cadranelle. It was far more expensive to live in the city than she had anticipated, and her money was disappearing fast. She still hadn't seen a doctor and she knew that for her unborn child's sake, she must do it soon.

The trouble was, she thought glumly, as she settled down for yet another long wait outside yet another personnel office, she had no qualifications, no credentials. Every opening seemed to call for either a degree or certificate of some kind or some documented experience.

Can you type? No. Do you have any references? No. Former employers? No. Social security number? No. Licenses, formal training? No.

It had rained all day, not a torrential downpour,

but the typical, never-ending drizzle of the North-west. Laurie had never minded that ceaseless mist in the islands, but the grey skies and dampness seemed gloomy and depressing in the maze of colourless buildings and paved streets of the city.

This was her last interview of the day, at Swedish Hospital. She had dressed with care in the morning in a navy blue woollen dress with white collar and cuffs, but by now her neat black pumps were soaked, her hair lifeless and damp and her dress rumpled.

She was ushered at last into a sanitary-looking room that reminded her more of her father's surgery than a business office except for the large wooden desk in front of the window.

A plump, middle-aged woman sat behind it, her iron-grey hair tortured into a tight knot at the back of her head, a severe pair of horn-rimmed glasses on her prominent nose. She peered over them sternly at Laurie.

'Sit down, Miss Cochran.'

In spite of the forbidding exterior, her voice was kind. Laurie glanced at the metal nameplate on the desk. Miss Flowers, it said, and she suppressed a hysterical giggle at the incongruity of the name.

They went through the same routine. Laurie's voice had developed a dull singsong quality from the constant repetition of the same old recitation of her lack of qualifications. No previous employment. No certificates. Blah, blah, blah.

She stood up to leave, sensing that she had come up against yet another stone wall.

'Just a minute,' said Miss Flowers. She hunted through a pile of papers on the desk. 'We do have one opening you might want to consider.' She hesitated. 'The pay isn't much, but it could work into something better.'

Laurie sat down carefully on the edge of her chair. 'I'd be willing to try almost anything,' she said quietly.

'Well, we do need someone to file X-rays. As I say, the pay is low, and it's boring work, but you can eat lunch in the cafeteria for practically nothing, and you'd be entitled to full medical benefits.' She smiled for the first time. 'Of course, being young and healthy, that may not be much of an incentive.'

If you only knew, Laurie thought to herself, just how much that does mean.

'Yes,' she said aloud, 'I'd like to try it.'

The next few months were relatively happy, peaceful ones for Laurie. Her new job was, indeed, dull, but she performed it conscientiously. She liked the rest of the staff, liked working in the busy hospital. She was grateful, in a way, that the work she did was not more taxing, since it gave her time to think and plan for the future.

Finally, in February, she did work up the courage to go to a doctor, choosing him carefully from the list of obstetricians at the hospital for his kind manner and fatherly appearance. Dr Patterson confirmed, of course, that she was indeed pregnant, about four months along.

As she had anticipated, he asked no questions about her marital status, assured her that he saw no problems ahead for her or the baby, and that there was no reason she couldn't continue to work until it was born.

Another month went by. March was wet and blustery, but with one or two sunny days, harbingers of the spring that was just around the corner. In the courtyard of the hospital a red camellia was blooming, and the daffodils were beginning to show a little colour on their tall fleshy stalks.

Laurie was five months pregnant by now, and although she had had to let out her few skirts to accommodate the growing thickness around her middle, no one would ever have suspected her condition. Besides, all the hospital employees had to wear shapeless, heavily starched white coats, the typical hospital uniform.

She had made a few friends at the hospital with whom she usually ate lunch in the cafeteria, but today she was eating late because of a rush job she had had to finish for one of the doctors who, typically, had to have those X-rays *now*!

She was just as glad to be eating alone. Although she felt well and the pregnancy was progressing normally, she found that she was more tired than usual. After her many years of quiet and near-solitude on Cadranelle, she found the constant presence of other people wearing.

It was two o'clock, and the cafeteria was almost empty. She sat at a table alone, and while she ate her tuna salad, she picked up the newspaper that was lying on the vacant chair next to her.

Glancing idly through it, with its usual fare of disasters and dire predictions for everything from peace to the economy, she suddenly saw, on the financial page, a picture of Miles Cutler.

She almost gagged on her salad. Coughing, she took a swallow of milk and eagerly bent her head to read the article below.

'Miles Cutler,' it said, 'well-known Metro troubleshooter, arrived back in Seattle late last night after five months of house arrest in Beirut, Lebanon. Mr Cutler, while in the Middle East to negotiate a loan with an Arab oil conglomerate, was accused by the Lebanese government of spying for the Israelis and detained while the case was being investigated. Although he refused to comment on the substance of the charges against him or the details of his release, Mr Cutler did say that he was not mistreated in any way and that the Lebanese government was most apologetic about the unwarranted detention.'

Laurie could only stare at the picture. It had been taken at the airport on his arrival, only last night. He was standing by his luggage at the baggage counter, dressed in a dark business suit, white shirt and tie.

He looked a little drawn, she thought, but otherwise exactly as she remembered him, the dark hair a little longer, but neatly combed, the tall lithe frame and air of reserved power in those dark eyes that gazed directly into the camera.

There were other people in the photograph, a reporter with a notebook, another holding a microphone, an official-looking, stern-faced man who could be a government official or bank executive.

And then there was the woman. She was tall, with long silky blonde hair that fell softly around a delicate-featured face to the upturned collar of a luxurious fur coat.

She was hanging on to Miles' arm and looking up at him with an expression mingled of adoration and possessiveness. Who could she be? Laurie wondered. He had said he wasn't married. His sister? No, he had said he had no family. His secretary?

What did it matter? All Laurie could think of was that Miles was here, here in Seattle, and that he hadn't abandoned her, broken his promise, as she had feared. The reason he hadn't contacted her, come back to her, was that he had physically unable to.

Her heart sang. Her one thought was to find him, to go to him. Now. Today. Nothing else mattered. He didn't even know she was in Seattle, and she must tell him right away.

She gathered up the newspaper and her handbag, hurried out of the cafeteria and went back to the X-ray library. There she told her immediate supervisor, a bored, unconcerned young man who was only biding his time in X-ray until he could get into medical school, that she had some urgent business to attend to and needed the rest of the afternoon off. He looked up from his magazine, yawned, and waved her off absently.

She would have to change her clothes, she thought excitedly as she walked the few short blocks from the hospital back to the Barclay. She knew where the Metropolitan Bank was, just a short bus ride down from Pill Hill to the city centre. She had gone by it many times in the hope of catching a glimpse of Miles.

Now, knowing she actually would see him soon, she felt as though her heart would burst with joy and relief. She hadn't been wrong about him, she thought as she dressed carefully in a neat dark suit and crisp white blouse. He hadn't broken his promise to her.

# CHAPTER FIVE

LAURIE's determination began to falter the moment she stepped inside the bank. It was so quiet, so sedate, so businesslike and imposing. She hesitated just inside the main entrance. To the left was the large bank proper, with its tellers' cages and tables in the centre for the customers' use. To the right were two elevators and a large black board with the names of officers and departments in small white letters.

Then she saw his name, and her heart began to pound wildly. Miles Cutler, Room 410. That would be the fourth floor. She got into the elevator. The heavy metal door shut noiselessly and she felt herself borne upward.

On the fourth floor she stepped out into a long, deserted corridor, heavily carpeted in a dark brown broadloom. The walls seemed to be solid marble.

She found room 410. There was a discreet bronze plaque on the heavy oak door. 'Business Extension Department,' it said. 'Miles Cutler, Vice-President.' Laurie opened the door and stepped inside into an elegant reception room.

There was the same rich brown carpeting, muted beige grass cloth on the walls, and several paintings. Her artist's eye recognised that they were original oils, landscapes, still lifes and one seascape.

The furniture was elegantly upholstered in a pale greyish-green, and there were mahogany tables with lamps, magazines and ashtrays. At one end of the long room there was a neat desk, and behind it a pleasant-looking middle-aged woman dressed in a discreet dark suit. She looked up from her typewriter.

'Yes?' she said to Laurie with a friendly smile. 'May I help you?'

Laurie felt a sudden surge of panic. What was she doing here? What would she say to Miles when she saw him? *If* she saw him? 'Hello, Miles, I'm carrying your baby'?

This office, with its imposing furnishings and air of forbidding elegance, was a totally alien setting for her meeting with Miles, out of the context of their time together on Cadranelle. Perhaps she should have called first, made an appointment or left a message.

Then she thought of her baby. Miles' baby. He had a right to know about it. The woman at the desk looked friendly, approachable, even maternal. The little wooden sign on the neat desk told Laurie her name was Mrs Ferrar. She noticed a spray of red camellias in a vase as she approached.

'I'd like to see Mr Cutler, please,' she said in a polite tone.

Mrs Ferrar smiled. 'Do you have an appointment? Mr Cutler is in a meeting at the moment.'

Laurie's heart sank. Of course, she thought, he

only got back last night. 'No,' she said, 'I don't.'

'Could you tell me what it's about?' Mrs Ferrar asked brightly. 'Perhaps someone else could help you, or I could speak to Mr Cutler about it and you could make an appointment to come back later.'

'I . . .' Laurie reddened, faltered, then plunged on. 'It's a personal matter,' she blurted out.

Mrs Ferrar raised neat plucked eyebrows just a fraction of an inch. She seemed to be thinking this over.

'Well,' she said at last dubiously, 'perhaps if you'd care to wait . . .'

She gestured towards a nearby chair. Laurie thanked her and sat down gingerly, and Mrs Ferrar returned to her typing.

As the minutes ticked by, Laurie's nerves began to give way again. The telephone rang constantly, and each time Mrs Ferrar said the same thing, her tone pleasant but firm. 'I'm sorry, Mr Cutler is in a meeting. Give me your name and number and I'll have him call you back.'

She picked up a magazine, a financial journal, and leafed absently through it with unseeing eyes, her mind firmly on the door behind Mrs Ferrar's desk, the door that must lead, she determined, to Miles' office.

Several people came and went, asking for Miles, and were politely turned away by the ever-vigilant Mrs Ferrar. A few got a warmer reception and passed beyond the protective desk to enter the inner sanctum beyond.

Finally, after an hour had passed, Laurie came to

the sad conclusion that she really had gone about this all wrong. In her excitement, she hadn't stopped to think. She knew now that she should never have come here like this. She would write to Miles or call him. She felt foolish and ill at ease in this strange atmosphere, out of place, an intruder.

She decided to tell Mrs Ferrar she wouldn't wait any longer and to give her her name and telephone number. Miles would call her as soon as he could, she knew.

Just as she rose to her feet, the door to the corridor opened and immediately the room was filled with the fragrance of an expensive perfume.

Laurie turned around to see the woman in the newspaper photograph with Miles striding towards the desk, the silky blonde hair swinging about her lovely face, the same fur coat draped casually over her shoulders.

'Hi, Margaret,' she called to Mrs Ferrar. 'Is Miles in? He's expecting me.' Her voice was cultivated, but with an edge of hardness. Her manner was totally self-assured. She didn't even glance at Laurie.

Mrs Ferrar was beaming. 'Oh, Miss Winthrop, how nice to see you again! Isn't it wonderful that Mr Cutler is back safe at last? He's in a meeting in the big conference room right now.' Her voice lowered confidentially. 'You know, all the bigwigs want to pick his brains about what happened over there. Why don't you go in and wait for him in his office?'

The blonde nodded briefly and confidently at her, then swept past the desk and through the door beyond.

Margaret Ferrar looked up at Laurie with excited eyes, misted over now with sentiment.

'That's Diana Winthrop,' she whispered loudly, 'Mr Cutler's fiancée. Isn't she beautiful? They make such a striking couple.' She babbled on, thrilled with the romance of the situation. 'They were to be married before he left, but then decided to wait until he got back. Because of the danger, you know. Thank heavens they did—she's been sick enough with worry as it is. I imagine we'll see a wedding soon, now, though.'

Laurie never knew how she got out of that office, down the elevator and into the busy street again. She must have blurted some excuse to Mrs Ferrar. She didn't care. In one stroke, her world had been shattered, her hopes dashed to the ground just when they had begun to rise again.

I was better off before I found out he'd come back, she groaned to herself on the trolley ride back up the hill to the Barclay. She felt sick and dizzy, barely able to navigate. At her stop, she stumbled off the trolley and across the street against a red light, oblivious to the angry shouts and honking horns.

Once inside the apartment, she threw herself on the couch and lay gazing blankly up at the ceiling, the excruciating shafts of pain shooting through her whole being, mind and body.

One agonising thought kept recurring, tormenting her. He was engaged to Diana Winthrop when he was at Cadranelle. He made love to me, knowing he was going to marry her. She could have forgiven him anything but that.

After what seemed like an eternity, she began to calm down. She got up and washed her face. It was dark out by now, raining again, a dismal, steady patter of drops against the window.

She made a pot of tea and sat at the kitchen table for a long time trying to think, to assess her situation, to decide what to do.

She hated Miles now. Oh, granted she had accepted him willingly, even eagerly. But would she have done so if she had known he belonged to another woman? Laurie had to admit she didn't know for sure, but she truly believed—she hoped—that if he had told her from the beginning that he was engaged to be married, she would never have allowed herself to nurture thoughts of love for him.

She got hungry around eight o'clock and had a bowl of soup. Finally, at ten, she fell, exhausted, into bed, her thoughts still churning. What should she do? What could she do?

When she awoke in the morning to the unfamiliar sun shining bleakly through the bedroom window, Laurie knew what she had to do. Everything had changed. She couldn't bear now to stay in the city where Miles lived. Miles and Diana.

The panic was gone. No more tears, she promised herself. No more grieving over what can't be helped. A hard knot of cold determination had formed in her heart.

After breakfast she went straight to the telephone and dialled the familiar number.

'Bendiksen Hotel,' came Emma's warm voice over the wire.

For a moment, the walls Laurie had built during the night threatened to crumble, but she quickly recovered.

'Emma,' she said firmly, 'it's Laurie.'

She heard a sharp intake of breath at the other end. Then, 'Laurie Cochran, where in the world have you been? I've been half worried out of my mind! I wanted to call the police, but Carl wouldn't let me. Where are you?'

'I'm in Seattle, Emma,' Laurie said when the flow finally ceased. 'I'm coming home—back to Cadranelle.'

'Well, thank the Lord!' Emma breathed devoutly. 'When?'

'In about two weeks. I'll call before I leave. Could Carl come to Sidney to pick me up?'

'Of course. Do you need anything?'

'No, I'm fine.' Laurie hesitated for a fraction of a second, then steeled herself and plunged on. 'I must tell you something, Emma. I'm pregnant.'

'Oh.' There was a short silence. 'Then . . .' Emma began in a timid voice, '. . . then . . . you mean . . . you got er—married?'

'No, Emma,' came the firm reply, 'I'm not married.'

Laurie had come to the painful conclusion during

the night that it was better to tell Emma before she went back. Give her time to get used to the idea, let her think it was someone she had met in Seattle.

'Well, dear,' came Emma's brisk voice, 'you're always welcome here, no matter what. You'll stay here at the hotel with us so we can look after you.'

Once again, Laurie almost broke down at this proof of her friend's love and understanding, and once again she made her heart go cold.

'We can talk about that when I get there,' she said. There was no point in arguing about that now. 'I'll call you in a few weeks, then, Em—and thanks for everything.'

After they had hung up, Laurie sat in the drab living room for a long time staring out of the window at the dreary brick wall of the building next door. I may have ruined my life, she thought, with my foolish gullibility, but at least I'll be back home where I belong.

Two weeks later, on a Friday, she was on the ferry headed for Sidney. It was a mild day. The water was clear, with only the steady flow of the tide to ruffle its surface.

Laurie stood silently at the railing on the upper deck throughout the whole trip, soaking in the salt tang of the air, listening to the familiar sounds of the gulls overhead, the hoot of an oncoming ferry, and gazing at the fathomless majesty of the blue sea.

It seemed that with the forward motion of the boat, she was leaving behind her a bad dream. As they passed by the islands of the San Juans through the narrow channels, the ugliness and dirt and crowded streets of the city seemed to drop from her mind as though they had never existed.

They docked briefly at Friday Harbor, and it crossed Laurie's mind that this was where her child would be born. She would have to get down to see Dr Finney soon, but there was no hurry.

Then they were out in the open straits, where the colour of the water changed, deepened, took on that greenish cast that was so like the colour of Miles Cutler's eyes. Once again she hardened her heart. As far as she was concerned, Miles Cutler was dead, had never existed.

She got off the boat at Sidney and went immediately through Customs. As she stood waiting patiently in line, her bags at her feet, she began to get the uneasy feeling that someone was staring at her.

She looked around the room. There at the table, processing entries, sat Officer Donaldson. He was looking straight at her, and when their eyes met, he smiled.

When her turn came he looked up at her, his expression serious and businesslike.

'Well, miss, so you did decide to come back. Is this a visit or a permanent return to your residence?' He grinned. 'That's an official question, not cheek!'

The sparkle in his clear blue eyes told her the question was quite as much personal as official. She smiled bleakly. If he only knew, she thought, that the girl he's chatting up is five months pregnant! She almost broke out laughing at the thought.

'It's permanent,' she replied in a clear firm voice. 'Quite permanent.'

'Well then,' he said cheerfully, stamping her form, 'we may meet again.'

For answer, Laurie only smiled and passed on. She picked up her bags and carried them out through the back of the terminal and started down the wooden staircase that led to the boat dock.

The bags seemed very heavy to her, and when she was halfway down the stairs, she stopped and set them down to rest for a moment. She looked down into the milling crowd below, hoping to catch sight of Carl. With the good weather, the ferry had been half an hour early. She might have to wait for him.

Then she heard someone call her name. She looked down, caught sight of a blond head shining in the sunlight, then stood, speechless, as Ted came bounding up the stairs towards her.

Of course, she thought. He was due back from Alaska at Christmas. As she watched him coming towards her, more slowly now, she froze. Had Emma told him about the baby? How could she face him? For a moment panic threatened, and she almost turned and ran back up the way she'd come.

But by then he was beside her, reaching for her bags. Laurie sighed. He would have to find out sooner or later. She hoped Emma had told him; it would be easier than having to do it herself.

'Hello, Ted.' She looked into his warm brown

eyes, and the hurt she saw there told her that he knew.

Was there no end to the repercussions of that one night of madness? She saw the years of struggle ahead of her, the pain she was causing others, her own loss of hope for happiness. All for one moment of stupid weakness.

'Hello, Laurie.' His expression was unreadable now, the brown eyes remote and cold. 'Carl couldn't come. He's been sick—A touch of 'flu.'

He turned from her then and started down the stairs with her suitcases. Laurie followed him, her eyes fixed firmly on the centre of the dark blue windbreaker covering his strong back.

Ted stowed her gear on his boat, jumped on to the deck, then left her to scramble aboard by herself. But although her pregnancy was still not outwardly apparent, the subtle changes in her body had dislocated her centre of gravity, and as she swung her legs over the side, she misjudged the distance, stumbled and almost fell.

Ted was beside her instantly, his hand grasping her elbow.

'Are you all right?'

She nodded. 'Yes, I'm fine. Just a little awkward.' She watched his face close up again. 'I haven't been on a boat for several months,' she explained. She knew that any reference to her condition would be hateful to him.

He grunted and turned away.

\*     \*     \*

The trip over to the islands was a rough one, and it took all Ted's attention to keep the small boat on course amid the foaming whitecaps and treacherous tides. A grey pall hung over the sky, darkening the sea and sending down a damp mist.

Laurie sat on the bench across the stern, clinging to the deck railing for safety as they made their bumpy way across the straits. She wasn't worried, even though they were rocked about unmercifully, but eventually her stomach began to rebel. Ted was an excellent sailor; if there had been any real danger he would never have risked the trip.

Fighting down her nausea, she thought that her only real concern was Ted and his utter rejection of her. She couldn't blame him. He had loved her, wanted to marry her, had set her up on a pedestal which she had now tumbled from with a vengeance. Of course he would hate her, just as she hated Miles. She could hardly blame Ted for his resentment now that she had tasted the bitter fruit of betrayal herself.

She watched him now at the helm, skilfully piloting the boat towards home. Home, she thought, closing her eyes. But would it still be home for her? What kind of reception would she get now that she was coming back in disgrace?

Just as her nausea was on the point of becoming unbearable, they left the straits and entered the narrow channel that led to the sheltered harbour of Cadranelle. Laurie's tense stomach muscles relaxed and she stood up. It was safe now to move about. She would have to help Ted tie up the boat and put the fenders out.

This time she eased herself over the side more carefully, and as she made the stern line fast around the heavy metal cleat on the dock, she heard the motor shut off and Ted jump on the platform to haul and secure the forward line.

Then suddenly he was beside her, his hands gripping her shoulders so hard she almost cried out in pain. She gave him a swift look. His face was tortured.

'Why, Laurie?' he ground out. 'Why?'

She lowered her eyes. 'Ted,' she said brokenly, 'forgive me.' Then she collected herself and looked up at him. 'I don't blame you for hating me—I hate myself. But it's done, and I can't change it.'

He closed his eyes, struggling for control. Then he sighed and dropped his hands from her shoulders.

'Come on,' he said gruffly. 'Emma's waiting.'

When they arrived at the hotel, Emma flew out of the door and down the front steps as fast as her short plump legs would carry her. She threw her arms around Laurie and held her tight.

'Oh, my dear, I'm so glad to see you again! I've been out of my mind with worry!' She held her at arm's length, then, and gave her a reproachful look. 'All those months and not a word. I didn't even know where you were, if you were alive or dead. Shame on you!'

Laurie almost broke down then, but she summoned up all the reserves of will power she could command and smiled.

'I'm sorry, Em. Forgive me. I couldn't call or write, not until . . .' She broke off. Not until I knew for sure, she thought, that Miles Cutler had betrayed my trust from the very beginning.

'Well, you're here now,' said Emma happily, leading her inside 'and that's all that matters. You'll stay with us,' she added firmly.

Laurie stopped short. 'No, Emma, I can't do that.'

'Why ever not?' Emma demanded. 'I want you here where I can keep an eye on you.' Laurie opened her mouth to protest, but Emma silenced her with a look. 'Come on, now. We'll have a cup of coffee—I just made a fresh pot.'

They sat in the warm, comfortable kitchen over the familiar table and Laurie told her all about her job, the drab apartment, the perils and pleasures of city life.

Ted had vanished soon after he had set her bags down just inside the door. Laurie hadn't even had a chance to thank him for coming to pick her up at Sidney. That was some unfinished business she would have to deal with eventually, she thought, as she recalled the hurt look in his eyes and his distant manner, but right now she was content to bask in the security and comfort of Emma's kitchen.

'Now,' said Emma firmly after they had finished their coffee, 'I don't want to hear any nonsense about your going off to live in your house all alone. You're staying here where I can look after you until the baby comes, at least, and that's final.'

'Oh, Emma—' Laurie began to protest.

'Now, you listen to me,' ordered Emma. She leaned across the table and put a plump hand on Laurie's arm. 'Debbie has gone off at last.' Laurie's eyes widened. Emma nodded abruptly, then sighed. 'Yes, she finally did it.' She got up and carried their cups to the sink. 'Carl says to leave her alone, that we can't lock her up.'

She turned around, her eyes misted over with tears. She drew a handkerchief out of the pocket of her shapeless cotton apron and blew her nose noisily.

'I think Carl is right,' Laurie said softly. She smiled wryly. 'I know I'm not a shining example of the results of freedom, but you can't keep her here against her will.'

'But she's so young!' wailed Emma.

'Age has nothing to do with it. Look at me, four years older, and see the mess I've gotten myself into. Debbie's tougher than I was—she'll be all right. I doubt if she'll make such a fool of herself over a man as I have.'

The two women stared at each other for a long moment. Laurie's gaze was hard, conveying the unspoken message that she did not want Emma's sympathy. Finally Emma turned again and began rinsing out the dishes.

'Well, at any rate,' she called over her shoulder, 'you'll be doing me a favour if you stay here at the hotel. With Debbie gone and Carl laid up, I could use an extra pair of hands.'

\*      \*      \*

It was settled finally that Laurie would stay at the hotel for a while, at least until Carl was back on his feet. There wasn't much activity in March anyway, only an occasional boater wanting groceries or a comfortable room for the night, or one of the boat tours stopping by for a meal.

Emma showed Laurie to her room that night after supper and helped her unpack. Each room had its own bath, so she would have all the privacy she wanted.

'Well, I'll say good night, then,' Emma called to her from the door. 'I'm so glad you're home again.' She started to leave, then stopped short and turned back. 'Oh, I almost forgot—a man called looking for you a few weeks ago.'

Laurie was sitting at the dressing table brushing her hair. Her hand paused in mid-air, and a cold chill clutched at her heart. Slowly she turned around.

'What man?'

'Let's see,' Emma went on, 'I wrote it down somewhere.' She fumbled in the pocket of her apron. 'It was a day or two after you called me. Of course, I didn't know how to get in touch with you. Ah, here it is,' she said, waving a crumpled piece of paper. 'Miles Cutler. He left a number for you to call if I heard from you.'

Laurie got up and walked slowly towards Emma, reaching for the paper. 'What did he say?' She could hardly trust her voice and prayed it didn't sound as shaky as she felt.

'Just that he'd called your house several times

and gotten no answer. He seemed quite worried, but of course I didn't know him from Adam and . . .'

'What did you tell him?' Laurie interrupted in a hard voice.

Emma gazed up at her in alarm. 'Why, I didn't tell him anything. Just that you'd left Cadranelle, and I didn't know where you were.' She gave Laurie a horrified look. 'Laurie, is he . . . ?'

Laurie's face was set. 'If Miles Cutler ever calls here again asking for me, Emma, please tell him that I'm not here and that you don't know where I am.'

Emma's face was troubled. 'Laurie, I'm a very bad liar.'

Laurie walked back to the dressing table and started to brush her hair again. 'That's all right, Emma. I don't think he'll be calling again.'

Emma started to say something, apparently thought better of it, and quietly left the room, shutting the door behind her.

Laurie sat for a long time, her body rigid, her face muscles set, brushing the silky black hair automatically. She glanced down at the crumpled piece of paper Emma had given her, still clutched in one hand.

There was only his name and two telephone numbers, one his office, the other his home. Slowly she wadded the paper up and threw it into the wastebasket.

# CHAPTER SIX

THE next morning, after breakfast, Laurie took a walk down to her house. The sky was overcast, but it was warm enough so that all she needed was a light sweater.

She drank in the freshness of the tangy salt air, breathing deeply, as if to expel the poison in her lungs from those months in the city. The trees were just beginning to leaf out in tender bright green shoots, and a blazing yellow forsythia bloomed by the front door.

The house was as she left it. Emma had turned on the heat and aired it out periodically so that there was no trace of mildew, that perennial blight of a damp climate.

As Laurie wandered through the familiar rooms, a fierce surge of love rose up in her, and she vowed she would never leave this place again. She would have her baby, make a life for herself, right here where she felt safe and protected. And she would do it alone.

Her painting gear was still in the downstairs hall closet where she had left it. It would soon be spring and she would be able to start painting outside again. Emma had said she would display her paintings this summer at the shop in the hotel, and maybe she could earn enough from them to keep herself and the baby.

There was a sudden sound from the front porch, a light rapping. Laurie froze, remembering the night of the storm when Miles had appeared at her front door, dripping wet, his arm covered with blood. Had he come back? She heard footsteps coming towards her down the hall and whirled around.

'Laurie?' It was Ted. 'I was walking by on the beach and saw the lights on,' he said gruffly. 'Thought I'd better take a look.'

Laurie slumped weakly against the closet door, then straightened up and carefully shut it. Her relief at seeing Ted was oddly mingled with disappointment. What if it had been Miles? Would he come looking for her? Of course not.

Yet he had called. She fought down the tiny spark of hope that thought kindled and turned warily to look at Ted. He stood before her, his eyes cast down, his hands in his trousers pockets. He looked at her and sighed.

'I want to apologise, Laurie, for the way I treated you yesterday.' She opened her mouth to protest, and he raised a hand. 'No, let me finish.' He ran a hand through his fair hair. 'I had no right to judge you. There was no excuse for the way I acted, especially when I know how rough it's been on you.' He made a helpless gesture with his hands and gave her a bleak look. 'You know, being pregnant and all.'

'Ted . . .' she began.

'Let me finish. Please.' He straightened his

shoulders. 'I am sorry—I want you to know that. It's just that . . . Hell, Laurie, you know how I've always felt about you. You wouldn't give me the time of day, and I always thought it was because you were—you know—too inexperienced or too pure for anything as crass as physical love. Then when Emma told me you were pregnant . . .' His hands tightened into fists at his side and his voice took on a hard edge. 'I wanted to kill you both.' He looked away.

Laurie knew it would be fatal to go to him now, to touch him, to try to comfort him. They had been friends for too long. She had always been honest with Ted about her feelings for him, and she wasn't going to start lying to him now in a feeble effort to justify herself or win his sympathy.

'Ted,' she said in a low voice, 'you can't be any sorrier about this than I am. But, as I said yesterday, it's done. There's nothing anyone can do to change it. I'm going to have this baby. I'm going to love it and raise it, and that's all there is to it.'

Ted gave her a fierce gaze, his brown eyes sullen and defiant. 'Who was he, Laurie? Just tell me that.'

Laurie turned away. 'No, Ted, I won't do that. Not ever.' She looked back at him, her eyes pleading. 'Can't you see I just want to forget about him, forget he ever existed?'

Ted started to make a move towards her, then checked himself. He put his hands back in his pockets and stood for a long time staring down at the floor. Then he lifted his head.

'Okay, put that way, I guess I can understand. God knows I'd like to forget about him, too.'

They stood in the hall facing each other for several moments, not speaking. Finally Ted broke the silence.

'We're leaving again tomorrow to go up north fishing. We'll be gone three or four months, depending on the weather. Maybe when I get back . . .' He shrugged.

'By then, Ted,' Laurie reminded him softly, 'the baby will be here.'

He clamped his jaw shut and gave her a stricken look. 'I know, I know. We'll just have to wait and see. But, damn it, I still love you, Laurie.'

He turned, then, and left. Laurie stood looking after him until he vanished from sight. She heard the front door close behind him, the sound of his boots as he walked across the porch and down the steps.

She sighed and put her hands over her face. Should she run after him? Tell him once again that a few months would make no difference, that she could never marry a man she didn't love?

Besides, she thought, who knew how she would feel by then? She valued Ted's friendship, was grateful for his forgiveness, his love. Wouldn't it be sensible to marry him if he still wanted her? It would be the solution to all her problems.

Still pondering, she locked up the house again and started back up the hill to the hotel. Ted was leaving tomorrow. When he came back, saw her with the baby, he might not want to marry her. She wouldn't blame him.

That afternoon Emma insisted that she take a nap. Laurie argued feebly, but she was tired, and one look in her dressing-table mirror at the drawn face and dark circles under her eyes convinced her that Emma was probably right.

It was quiet in the hotel. Carl was sleeping off the last stages of his illness in his own room down the hall, and Emma was outside getting an early start on her annual vegetable garden.

Laurie took off her denim pants and cotton shirt and laid them over a chair. Wrapping her black robe with the red poppies on it around her, she sat at the dressing table to comb out her hair. She hadn't finished putting all her things away yet, and when she reached for her comb on the cluttered dressing table, she knocked off a jar of shampoo into the wastebasket.

As she bent down to retrieve it, her eye fell on the crumpled paper she had thrown in there last night. She stared at it, and the little spark of hope she had smothered earlier began to kindle.

She felt her heart begin to pound wildly. He had tried to contact her, she thought. He had even gone so far as to call the hotel looking for her. After all, she was the one who had vanished. Wouldn't it be foolish not to even give him a chance to explain?

But how could he explain away Diana Winthrop and the fact that he was engaged to her? And what was even worse, had been engaged to her when he made love to Laurie. No, she thought, straightening up and giving her reflection in the mirror a cold stare, she could never forgive him for that.

Yet, engaged or not, he *had* called her as soon as he got back. Didn't that prove he cared something about her? Her eyes softened and she put her fingers lightly to her mouth, remembering the burning kisses Miles had placed there, the feel of that mouth on hers, demanding, thrusting.

She closed her eyes. She felt suddenly weak and dizzy, and gripped the edge of the table lightly. All that passion, all that love, she thought, that total giving of herself. Was she going to waste it because of a stiff-necked pride?

Finally she made up her mind. She reached down and retrieved the piece of paper, glancing at the telephone numbers. It was Sunday; he would most likely be at home.

Her pulses racing, she flew down the corridor to the front desk where the telephone was kept. She smoothed out the paper on the hard surface, took a deep breath, lifted the receiver, and with trembling fingers began to dial.

As the telephone rang in her ear, her knees grew weak and she sank down on the tall stool Emma used at the desk. It rang five times, then six. Just as Laurie was about to hang up, there was a sharp click at the other end.

'Hello, Cutler residence,' came a familiar feminine voice. Laurie couldn't speak. 'Hello,' the voice repeated. 'Is anyone there?'

It was Diana Winthrop. There was no mistaking

that confident tone, the clipped aristocratic in-flection. Or was it Diana Cutler by now? Laurie wondered as she slowly replaced the receiver.

She dragged herself wearily back to her room, shut the door and lay down on the bed. She lifted an arm to cover her eyes.

I will not cry, she promised herself fiercely. Nothing has changed. There was one slight chance, and I took it. Now I'm back where I started. I could manage then, and I'll manage now.

She moved her arm to her side and lay for a long time staring up at the ceiling, dry-eyed, fighting off thoughts of Miles and Diana. Miles and Diana.

Finally, exhausted, she drifted off into a troubled sleep.

The days passed quickly. Determined to keep her-self busy, Laurie helped Emma at the hotel in the mornings, then went home to paint in the after-noon. She took long walks up and down the beach every day, and by evening she was so tired she would fall into bed by nine o'clock.

She began making monthly visits to Dr Finney in Friday Harbor, and it was arranged that she would spend her last week before the baby was due at his house. His wife, too, was an ex-nurse, and had been a great friend of Laurie's mother. The actual birth would take place in the tiny hospital.

Dr Finney assured her that she would breeze right through the rest of her pregnancy and actual childbirth with no problems. She was young and healthy, and the baby's heartbeat was strong.

Gradually, as the weather warmed and her body changed to accommodate the growing life within, something like peace began to come to her. Her painting was going well. By the middle of June Emma had already sold the three seascapes she had painted since her return in March, and she was hard at work on another one. Emma had convinced her that since they sold so well, she should raise the price.

The baby was due in three weeks now. It was arranged that Carl would take her down to Friday Harbor when the time came. She had made up her mind that when she came back she would return to live in her own house again. She was grateful for Emma's care and knew it was better for her not to be alone right now, but she longed for her own home.

Once the tourist season got under way, after Memorial Day, at the end of May, the hotel was constantly busy. Laurie helped as much as she could, taking on most of the chores that would keep her out of the public eye. She had come to terms with her pregnancy and no longer felt ashamed of it, but her unwieldy body made her shy of the stares of strangers.

So far, after that one telephone call three months ago, she had managed to fight back all thoughts of Miles Cutler. When there was no hope, you simply did what you had to do. Ted would be back soon, and she wondered if that would lead anywhere. Through this difficult period, they had both probably grown up a little.

Mondays were particularly busy at the hotel, and Laurie was kept hopping all morning turning out the recently-vacated rooms. This particular Monday was a fine June day, and she opened all the windows wide to air out the rooms while she vacuumed and dusted.

By noon she had finished all the cleaning. She was tired, hungry and grimy. She'd take a shower, she decided, then have lunch. When she glanced out the open window she could see that a mass of black clouds was drifting in from the south. It would rain soon. Better shut the windows.

She went back through the row of rooms fastening the windows. There were already a few drops of rain on them. As she came back to the room closest to the front of the hotel, she glanced outside towards the front porch. She gasped and looked again.

Miles Cutler was striding up on to the porch. Laurie's heart skipped several beats and she had to grasp the windowsill to keep from falling. She was terrified that he might see her, but a powerful force kept her at the window, her eyes riveted on the tall man not thirty feet away from her.

He stood on the porch for a while, under cover, and Laurie could see the scowl of his handsome face. He was so tall, she thought, as she fought to gain control of herself, so imposing-looking with his shock of black hair and powerful build. He was dressed in black trousers and a grey poplin windbreaker. As he bent over, cupping his hands to light a cigarette, the material strained against his hard-muscled back and shoulders.

Trembling, Laurie moved away from the window to hide behind the curtain. She took deep breaths, struggling for control. Still she couldn't take her eyes off him. He turned around then, and with a puzzled frown looked directly into her window.

Could he see her? No, not now that she was behind the curtain. What was he doing here? Was Diana with him? Gradually Laurie began to come to her senses again. Her one thought was that Miles must not see her, not in her condition. She knew that eventually she might have to face him, but not now, she prayed, not looking like a baby blimp.

Quickly she ran into the corridor and down to her own room, slamming and locking the door behind her. She leaned back against it, still trembling. What should she do?

The agonising thing was that just the sight of him brought it all back to her again. Every detail she had thought she had managed to erase from her mind flooded back in—all their moments together, all the pain of his betrayal, and worse, all her love for him.

She lay down on the bed, fighting off the tears. She would not cry for him again, she vowed. She lay there, rigid, for what seemed like hours, listening to the gentle rain pattering on the windowpane, staring blankly at the ceiling.

Finally she could endure it no longer. Awkwardly, she swung her legs over the side of the bed and sat up. She glanced at her watch. It was one o'clock.

Only an hour had passed. It had seemed like a day, an eternity.

There was a light tap at the door, and Laurie put her hand to her throat. Would Emma have let him come to her room? She couldn't hide in here for ever.

'Yes?' she said in a strangled voice.

'It's me—Emma.'

Laurie got up and walked slowly to the door. Then, sighing fatalistically, she opened it. Emma stood there, alone, her eyes wide. She stepped inside.

'It's that man,' she whispered. 'The one who called when you were in Seattle—Mr Cutler.'

'Did you tell him I was here?' Laurie's voice was harsh.

'No. No, I didn't.' Emma was wringing her plump hands, in obvious distress. 'He just asked if you'd come back to your house. Said he'd been down there and hadn't seen any sign of life.'

Thank God, Laurie breathed to herself, she had stayed at the hotel. If she'd moved back in the house she would have had to face him. It was sheer luck that he'd come in the early afternoon. A few more hours and she would have been down there painting.

'Well, Emma,' she said, forcing out a smile, 'at least you didn't have to lie.'

'No. But somehow it felt like lying.' Emma gave Laurie an unhappy questioning glance. 'Laurie, I know you don't want to talk about it, and it's none of my business, but he seems like an awfully nice man. And really quite concerned about you. I'd say he was also a proud man who doesn't show his feelings easily, but at one point he seemed quite angry, said he didn't see how anyone could just drop out of sight that way.' She paused, then added, 'He's very handsome.'

'Yes,' Laurie said bitterly, 'he's very nice, very handsome. Tell me, did he say he'd brought his wife along with him?'

Emma gave a little gasp and put her hand to her mouth. 'Oh, Laurie! I didn't realise . . .' She put a hand on Laurie's arm. 'You poor little thing . . .' she began kindly.

Laurie closed her eyes tight. 'Don't, Em,' she begged. 'Please, no sympathy.'

Emma quickly withdrew her hand. 'No, no, of course not.' She sighed. 'Well, I don't think he'll be bothering you again. He only stopped to buy some groceries. He's on his way up north, up to the Powell River to do some fishing. Said he'd be gone a month or more.'

'He's gone, then?' asked Laurie with relief.

Emma nodded. Well, Laurie thought, that was that. She prayed it was the last time Miles Cutler would ever set foot on Cadranelle.

Still, as she lay in bed that night, she couldn't help wondering why he had ever bothered to ask for her. Possibly because he didn't seduce that many virgins, she thought bitterly, and the episode stood out in his mind.

Then she remembered the real circumstances of their affair, how he had wanted to go that night and she had done everything in her power to keep him with her, and she knew she wasn't being fair to blame him entirely.

He was gone now, out of her life for good. Perhaps one day, if she ever saw him again by chance, she might be able to face him without the pounding heart and weak knees. Perhaps . . .

## CHAPTER SEVEN

LAURIE'S baby was born in mid-July—a boy. She named him James, after her father, and called him Jamie. He was a healthy baby, and although it was too soon to tell for sure, she thought she could see flecks of blue-green in his eyes.

She stayed in the small hospital at Friday Harbor for three days. It had been an easy delivery, and she was anxious to get home, to start caring for Jamie on her own.

On the morning she was to leave, she dressed in the normal clothes she had brought with her to go home in, a simple blue cotton shirtwaister. It had been a warm July, and the sleeveless dress would be just right for the trip home.

As she packed her things, wondering when Carl would show up to get her, she heard a light tap on the open door behind her. She turned around and saw Ted standing there, a sheepish, hesitant look on his face.

'Ted!' she explained, taken by surprise. 'You're back.'

He came into the room. 'We got back last week.' His voice was stiff and formal.

Laurie smiled at him. She was determined to be natural with him. 'Did you have a good catch?'

He nodded. There was a short strained silence.

116

Laurie turned and resumed her packing.

'What happened to Carl?' she asked over her shoulder. 'Not sick again, I hope.'

She heard him take a step towards her and steeled herself.

'Laurie . . .' he began, his voice low and throbbing with emotion.

At that moment the nurse came bustling in with the baby.

'Here we are, Laurie,' she said with a wide grin. 'Think you can handle this young man all by yourself?' She nodded curtly at Ted, giving him a suspicious look, and placed the tiny bundle in Laurie's arms. 'He eats like a horse, you know. I've packed some of his formula for you, and a list of instructions.'

The minute Laurie took Jamie in her arms, she was lost to anything or anyone else. He was asleep, and she looked down at him tenderly, lovingly.

Smiling, without stopping to think, she glanced up at Ted, her joy visibly apparent on her shining face, but when she met his fierce angry glare, her blood ran cold, her joy dampened. Of course, she thought, he would naturally be resentful.

'We'd better get going,' he said curtly. He picked up her suitcase off the bed and turned away from her.

Ted had borrowed a car from a friend at Roche Harbor, at the northern tip of San Juan Island, just across the narrow channel from Cadranelle, leaving his boat moored at that busy resort. It was a much faster trip by car than by boat, and by the middle of summer the road up through the centre of the big island was in good repair.

The drive from Friday Harbor to Roche Harbor was a silent one. Ted had not even glanced at Jamie. It was as though if he refused to acknowledge him, the baby would somehow cease to exist.

His attitude hurt Laurie, but was no more then she expected. She couldn't blame him. She could empathise entirely with the feeling of loss and betrayal he must be experiencing, and at least she had her baby. She could hardly take her eyes off him.

She was grateful, however, when they finally arrived at Roche Harbor. The little village was thronged with tourists, whole families wandering idly through the town, enjoying the warm weather and remote island setting. The water sparkled, and the tall pointed steeple of the little white church on the bluff overlooking the harbour shone in the summer sunshine. An enormous flock of bright blue-green swallows cut symmetrically through the clear blue sky.

They left the car at Ted's friend's house and walked the few blocks to the busy marina down below. When they reached Ted's boat, the last one in a long line, Laurie began to worry about how she was going to get on board with Jamie. She was physically able to manage by herself, but not holding the baby, too.

Ironically, the heretofore placid Jamie chose just

that moment to wake up and start crying. Rocking him gently in her arms, Laurie gave Ted an apprehensive look.

'He's hungry,' she explained weakly. 'I'll feed him as soon as I get on board.'

Ted only stared silently, not moving a muscle to help her. Laurie cleared her throat.

'I'm very sorry, Ted,' she said loudly over the cries of the now screaming baby, 'but you're going to have to help me.' She was beginning to grow angry at Ted's stubborn silence. He didn't *have* to come to get her, after all.

Ted only gave her a startled look and continued to stare.

'Here,' she said finally, thrusting the noisy, red-faced Jamie at him. 'It won't hurt you to hold him for two seconds while I get on board. He won't bite.'

She almost laughed at the shocked expression on Ted's face when he found himself with the crying baby in his arms. As quickly as she could, Laurie eased herself carefully over the side of the boat, then reached out her arms for the baby.

Miraculously, he had stopped crying. With wide eyes, Laurie looked up at Ted, who seemed to be just as astounded at this development as she was. He glanced down at the baby, then at Laurie, and smiled.

'He's awfully little to have made such a racket,' he commented.

Then, with a puzzled frown on his face, he handed the baby to her. Seeming to sense that this meant food at last, Jamie set to yowling again immediately.

Laurie took him down into the cabin, changed him and warmed his bottle. By the time she had finished all her ministrations to her demanding son, they had crossed the channel and were bumping gently against the dock at Cadranelle.

Laurie went back up on deck, and saw Emma standing at the dock waiting eagerly. When she caught sight of Laurie with the baby, she gave a little cry and held out her arms. Smiling, Laurie handed the bundle to her.

This time Ted helped her gently over the railing and on to the dock. She was grateful for the support of his strong arms as he lifted her, suddenly realising how tired and weak she really felt.

Emma had already started up the hill with the baby, cooing and clucking, and when Ted set Laurie down on the dock, he held her for some moments longer than necessary. Puzzled, Laurie looked up at him. His face was troubled, as though he was trying to work out a difficult problem.

'Laurie,' he said, releasing her at last. He hesitated, seemed to struggle inwardly, then gave her a sheepish grin. 'It's a nice baby.'

Laurie cocked her head on one side and returned his smile. 'The feeling seems to be mutual,' she remarked lightly. 'I must remember to call on you whenever Master James decides to throw a tantrum!'

*   *   *

After a short, but tiring visit at the hotel, where all the island neighbours had to come in to get a look at the baby, including several gaping tourists caught up in the spirit of the thing, and over Emma's vehement objections, Laurie announced that it was time for her to go home.

'I don't see why,' said Emma tearfully. 'You can stay here for ever if you want to.'

'Emma,' Laurie explained gently, 'you know I planned to go back home as soon as the baby came. I can still come up in the morning to help you in the hotel.'

'No need,' Carl put in gruffly. 'You tend to that young man of yours and get on with your pictures. With Debbie coming back, we'll do fine.'

Laurie's eyes widened. 'Debbie's coming back?' She turned to Emma. 'Oh, Em, I'm so glad!'

Emma beamed. 'Not half as glad as I am. You and Carl were right—a few months of freedom and city life, and she's happy enough to come back where she belongs.'

She finally surrendered the baby, who was beginning to show signs of dampness, and Laurie and Ted went off down the hill to her house.

'I put your dinner in the fridge,' Emma called after them.

Laurie turned and waved. 'Thanks again for everything!'

Laurie had turned her father's old bedroom into a nursery. The neighbours had donated used baby furniture, and Laurie had painted it and made new curtains.

While she took Jamie inside and tended to his needs, Ted brought her suitcase up and put it in her room. She laid the baby in his new crib and went out on the landing to meet Ted.

'Thanks for everything, Ted,' she said with a weary smile.

'Is there anything else you need?' he asked.

'No. I'm just tired now. I'll manage all right on my own after I've had some dinner and a good night's sleep.' She laughed. 'That is, as much as His Lordship will allow me.'

'I'll be going, then.' He hesitated at the top of the stairs. 'I'm glad you're back, Laurie,' he said at last. 'Even with the little screamer.'

He turned then and went down the stairs.

During the next several weeks, Laurie established a busy but pleasant daily routine for herself, all, of course, revolving around little Jamie.

Once they settled in, he turned out to be an amazingly good baby, rarely crying except when he was hungry. He soon gave up his night feedings, and Laurie's strength returned quickly.

Ted came over almost every day, and they fell into an easy relationship similar to the one they had had before Miles came into her life. After the initial brief rejection, he had come to accept the baby easily and even seemed quite fond of him.

Once or twice, Laurie had sensed a conversation drifting beyond friendship. A certain look would appear on Ted's face, a softening of the warm brown eyes, and she knew intuitively that with the slightest encouragement, his friendship for her would blossom into romance, perhaps even lead to thoughts of marriage again.

She had thought the matter over carefully and come to the conclusion that she couldn't give him that encouragement. Whenever she sensed his thoughts turning in that direction, she quickly changed the subject. Not only did it seem unfair to her to saddle him with another man's child, but she knew beyond a doubt that as much as she valued his friendship, she could never love him the way he deserved to be loved.

As time passed, she became more and more convinced that she could never love anyone again the way she had loved Miles. What was more, she didn't want to. He had spoiled her for ever for any other man, for anything less.

One of the first things she did after they were settled was to go through her painting things. Emma told her she was sure she could sell everything she painted, and that several people had asked to see her work.

One day in early August, Ted helped her sort out her painting things from the hall closet and set up her easel outside. As they were rummaging through the stacks of canvases, they came upon the portrait of her father.

'Say, this is really good,' said Ted, seizing it and holding it up. He gave her an appreciative glance. 'Looks just like him. And the colours are terrific.'

He put a finger on the sea in the background. 'You got that just right. Aren't you going to have it up?'

'Why, yes, I guess I should. I'd forgotten it.' Laurie looked at it and a host of warm memories of her father swept through her. She set it aside. 'I'll put it up in the big room upstairs over the fireplace.'

Ted had lifted out a pile of sketchbooks and was leafing through them, commenting admiringly on each one as he recognised familiar faces and landmarks. Then suddenly he stopped. Laurie glanced over at him to see what had caught his attention. He was staring fixedly down at the book in his lap.

'Who's this?' he asked in a hard voice.

He thrust the sketchbook at her. Puzzled, Laurie looked down. It was a page of several sketches she had done of Miles. In one, he was laughing, his head thrown back, a white shirt open at the neck, revealing the long column of his throat. In another, his expression was serious, pensive, a shock of dark hair falling over his forehead. In yet another, the dark eyes were brooding and alight with passion.

Laurie flushed deeply as recollection came flooding back. These pencil sketches of Miles clearly and unequivocally revealed exactly how she had felt about him, exactly what their relationship had been.

Her face flaming, she gave Ted a stricken look. His eyes were hard, his mouth set.

'He's the one, isn't he, Laurie?'

She nodded dumbly. 'Yes,' she whispered, dropping her eyes. 'He's the one.'

'Who is he? What's his name?' Ted's voice was vicious. 'I'll kill him!'

'Oh, Ted,' she pleaded, 'don't talk like that. What difference does it make? He's out of my life for good. I don't want to talk about it, don't want to be reminded of it.'

She tore the sheet from the book and ripped it to shreds. 'There,' she said, wadding the tiny pieces up in her hand. 'Now, let's forget it.'

Ted got to his feet and looked down at her. 'I don't know, Laurie. I don't know if I can.'

He turned, then, and walked out. Wearily Laurie rose to her feet. Maybe it's better this way, she thought, as she slowly climbed the stairs. There's no future for Ted with me anyway.

She threw the torn remains of her sketches of Miles into the fireplace and put a match to them. As she watched them burn, she kept repeating over and over again, 'This is the end at last.'

Ted stopped by a few days later, penitent and shamefaced. He told Laurie that he and his father were taking the boat up the Straits of Juan de Fuca to Neah Bay at the tip of Cape Flattery to do some ocean fishing for a few weeks. They were leaving right away and he just wanted to say goodbye.

Laurie was grateful that they were to be friends again, but relieved to see him go off for a while. Seeing those sketches of Miles had shaken her more than she would have dreamed, and she needed some time alone to get her bearings again.

After lunch, she settled Jamie in his crib upstairs

for his afternoon nap and went out into the clearing to work on her painting. She had found that her work was by far the best medicine for the dull ache in her heart that never quite left her. Once she became absorbed in trying to recapture on canvas the colours and shapes of the islands, she forgot everything else.

She was trying something new in this latest picture. All her paintings had sold so well that she thought it was time to experiment. The others she had done were too stiff, too stereotyped, carefully and lovingly done, but without any originality. They didn't quite express her unique and quite individual feeling for Cadranelle.

She had decided to blur the background on this picture and to focus the eye on a battered old rowboat that had been beached on the rocks below her house for as long as she could remember. She was aiming for a more impressionistic effect, and was excited about trying it.

It was a fine day, warm and a little sultry. Laurie had showered after lunch and put on a loose yellow cotton shift that buttoned down the front. She had given up make-up altogether, and her face glowed with a healthy rosy tan.

She worked steadily for about an hour, totally absorbed in her work, her black silky hair falling loosely about her face as she concentrated. Finally she sat back in her camp chair and squinted critically at what she had done so far.

It wasn't quite right, she thought to herself, but it was close. Frowning, she took up her brush and began gently to smear the paint she had just applied, tentatively at first, then more boldly as she saw her original intention begin to take shape on the canvas before her eyes.

She was so excited about her discovery that she didn't hear the footsteps until a dry branch snapped loudly, cracking through the stillness.

She glanced up over her easel. There, to one side, by the clump of birches, stood Miles Cutler. She drew in her breath sharply, so startled she almost fell off her chair.

For a long moment they simply stared at each other across the twenty feet or so that separated them. Laurie fought for control. Part of her wanted to run into the house and slam the door shut against his sudden presence, and part of her wanted to go to him and throw herself into his arms. For now some powerful force kept her glued to her chair, her eyes riveted on the tall man before her.

She was, quite simply, struck dumb, left breathless by his sheer physical beauty. He was standing as he had stood the last time, one arm resting on the white trunk of a birch tree, the other hanging at his side.

He looked so tall standing there, so strong. He was wearing dark trousers that moulded his slim hips and long powerful legs. His white shirt was open at the neck, and his gold watch gleamed in a shaft of sunlight.

He looked tanned and fit, his dark hair longer now, after two months away from civilisation. His eyes were narrowed at Laurie, the heavy dark brows creased in a frown. The still air seemed to crackle with electricity as they stared at each other wordlessly.

'Miles,' she managed to say at last. She tried to force a casual smile, but the muscles of her face had gone rigid with the shock of seeing him.

He took one step towards her, and her eyes widened in fear. She put a hand to her throat. Then he was walking slowly towards her, his hands on his hips, his eyes smouldering. He stood over her.

'Where in the hell have you been?' he ground out harshly, glowering down at her.

Laurie had had time to recover herself by this time. The pain she had suffered through in silence since she last saw him had strengthened her and came to her rescue now. She was determined to make use of that strength.

Carefully, she put her brush down on the easel and looked up at him. Her heart was still racing, but she had managed to gain control of her facial muscles at last.

'Don't shout at me,' she said calmly.

'I'm not shouting!' he roared. 'I just asked you a simple question. Answer me—where have you been?'

Laurie picked up her brush and leaned down to put it in the jar of turpentine at her feet, stalling him, fighting for time. Then she felt a large strong hand grip her bare arm and pull her roughly to her feet.

'Damn it,' he rasped, 'answer me!'

They were so close now that she could feel his

warm breath on her face, see the little pulse throbbing angrily at his jaw, the dark shadow of his
beard. She looked away, wincing.

'You're hurting me,' she protested.

She was beginning to grow frightened. The Miles
she had known had been gentle and loving. She had
sensed in him then the presence of tremendous
power kept in check, and loved him for it. Now that
power seemed to be unleashed against her, and she
could barely keep from trembling.

'You're damned right I'm hurting you,' he
growled, tightening his grip on her arm. 'And I'll
keep on hurting you until you answer my question!'

Why was he so angry? she began to wonder.
What had he expected? That she would run to him
and throw her arms around him, welcome him back
into her life, her heart, as if nothing had happened?

She thought of all those months alone, facing a
bleak empty future with an illegitimate child. She
thought of Jamie upstairs asleep in his crib, of Ted
who was so forgiving and loving. If anyone has a
right to be angry, she thought, it's me. Her one
thought was to protect her child and the life she was
building so painfully.

She glared up at him, coldly furious now. 'Just
what gives you the right to question me?' she asked
in a hard voice.

Miles' eyes widened in shock, and it was all she
could do to keep from drowning in those deep
blue-green pools. His hold on her loosened and he
heaved a deep sigh.

'What's wrong, Laurie?' he asked in a low voice.

She turned her head away. 'No, look at me!' he barked, forcing her head back. 'I've been half out of my mind for months searching for you. I promised you I'd come back. Now tell me what's wrong.'

What could she say? How could she tell him that she knew about Diana without sounding possessive and petty? She had no rights where he was concerned. She glanced at his left hand. There was no ring there. He had tried to find her after all. Maybe she'd been wrong about him.

She looked up at him, her face troubled, debating within herself. Maybe there was an explanation. She bit her lip, unsure of herself now. He was waiting.

'Miles, I . . .' she began.

Then their eyes met, and she knew she was lost. She watched, transfixed, as his dark head bent slowly towards her. She closed her eyes. His arms came around her and she felt his lips on hers.

She slumped against him with a sigh, her bones like water, and he held her to him fiercely. His mouth became more insistent as it ground against hers, and she tasted the salty tang of her own blood.

She threw her arms around his neck, then, arching her body closer to him, tangling her fingers in the thick dark hair at the back of his neck. His hands moved feverishly up and down her back, the thin material of her shirt sliding sensuously over her bare skin under his touch.

He put his hands on her hips and pulled her closer, so that she could feel his male hardness, unmistakable evidence of his growing desire. She opened her lips and gasped under his kiss as he probed her mouth. One hand was at her breast now, stroking and kneading. She groaned aloud.

Miles tore his mouth from hers and looked down into her eyes, one hand still moving on her breast, the other holding her tightly to him.

'I want you, Laurie. Now. As I've always wanted you. God, how I've wanted you all these months!'

His hands came up to cup her face. He looked deeply into her eyes. Then, as his hold on her tightened possessively and she was ready to give him anything he asked of her, her mother's ear caught the first faint gurgling sounds of Jamie awakening from his nap.

Jamie! She had almost forgotten him. She stiffened. Had Miles heard? Her body grew cold and rigid, and she pulled away from him. What was she doing here in the arms of this man? A man, she thought bitterly, who belonged to another woman.

He sensed the tension and withdrawal in her and dropped his hands, frowning. 'What is it?' he asked in a puzzled tone.

Laurie never knew, afterwards, where the strength came from for what she had to do. Perhaps the months of pain had hardened her. She only knew that she must resist this compelling man who had so much power over her, that if she gave in now to her desire for him, she would be lost again, back to where she was before, and that the security she had built up would vanish.

'I want you to leave here, Miles,' she ground out in a hard voice, 'and never come back.' He reached out a hand, his face stunned. She flinched. 'No,' she shouted, 'don't touch me!'

His hand dropped to his side and he held her eyes in his for a long moment. Laurie felt as though she was being torn limb from limb. Her whole body ached with longing to reach out to him, to gather him to her breast, but her gaze never faltered.

'Why, Laurie?' he asked finally. 'What's happened? You said you loved me once.'

'I was a child then,' she snapped. 'You said it yourself. Well, I've grown up, thanks to you. I'm a woman now, and as a woman I have the right to choose who makes love to me!'

He gave her a strange look from under a thunderous brow. A muscle at his jaw twitched, and Laurie knew he was barely containing his anger.

'I think I preferred you as a child,' he said at last in a tone of contempt.

'I'm sure you did, Miles,' she retorted with a harsh laugh. 'I was a real pushover then, wasn't I?'

They stood glaring at each other. Laurie sensed his growing fury. He looked as though he wanted to hit her. But she raised her chin defiantly, determined not to back down.

His eyes dropped, then, to her breast, heaving in anger, swelling above the low bodice of her shift.

'I'm not going to beg, Laurie,' he said in a clipped voice. 'I'm not one of your island boys you can play with, tease along and then slap down.' A gleam appeared in the dark eyes. 'You are a woman now, aren't you? So I needn't have any scruples then about offending your delicate girlish sensibilities.'

His eyes grew hard again. 'Now, damn it, I want an explanation. I want to know where you've been and why you're putting on this frigid act with me.' His hard fingers bit into her shoulders. 'Answer me!' he shouted.

'All right,' she shouted back, 'I will!' She glared at him with fire in her eyes, past caring now what she said. 'Did you bring your wife with you?' Her voice was clear and controlled.

His whole body went rigid. 'My wife? I have no wife.'

She saw the look of shock in his eyes. He dropped his hands from her shoulders as if burned and stepped back a pace.

She turned and walked away from him, puttering needlessly with her brushes and paints. 'Oh, have you and Diana postponed your wedding again?' she asked coolly, her back to him. 'When is it to be, then?'

The tension in the air was palpable. Despite her calm exterior and even tone, Laurie's heart was thundering within her. Still, she remained fiercely determined to see this through to the end. She had nothing to lose, and it had to be settled one way or the other.

She turned to face Miles. He stood there, his hands in his trousers pockets, staring out at the sea. His face was expressionless, his jaw set. Finally he sighed heavily and turned to her.

'How did you find out?' he asked wearily.

'About Diana?' Laurie kept her voice light. She laughed and looked away. 'What difference does it make? I know you were engaged to her before, when you made love to me.'

'Tell me how you found out,' he repeated.

'All right, I will. I was in Seattle when you came back from Lebanon. I read about it in the paper, saw the picture of you together. I knew then that you hadn't come back as you'd promised because you couldn't.' She hesitated.

'That's right,' he said in a cold voice. She waited, but apparently he wasn't going to say anything more. She lifted her chin, anger rising in her again as she recalled that humiliating trip to his office the next day.

'I went to your office.' His eyes widened, and she laughed again. 'Yes, the little green country girl acted true to form. I realise now how stupid that was, especially when Diana Winthrop came in, while I was waiting to see you and I found out you were engaged to her.' Her voice faltered. 'That you'd been engaged to her when you were here with me on Cadranelle.'

Miles made an angry sound deep in his throat. 'God,' he ground out, 'so that's why you disappeared!'

He turned his head so that she saw only the clean lines of his profile. He's not married, she thought to herself with a little surge of joy. She longed to reach out to him, to lay her hand on the flat plane of his cheek, to place her fingers on his lips.

He ran a hand through his crisp black hair, tousling it so that it fell in disorder over his forehead.

'I should have told you about Diana,' he said slowly. 'Everything happened so fast. I needed time to think.'

'*You* needed!' she hurled at him, angry again. 'What about my needs? Time ran out on me.'

He gave her a questioning look. 'What do you mean by that? I didn't exactly rape you, you know. It seemed to me you were quite willing. I hardly forced myself on you, if you'll recall.'

'Please don't remind me,' she said bitterly. 'Believe me, I've had plenty of reasons to regret my weakness and stupidity.' She gave him a steady look. 'But it would never have happened if I'd known you belonged to another woman.'

He lifted one heavy eyebrow and gave her a hard glare. 'Oh, wouldn't it?' His voice was mocking. 'Are you so sure about that? It seems to me you responded to me quite willingly and ardently just a few minutes ago.' She flushed deeply. 'And remember this,' he went on, 'I don't *belong* to anyone.'

His hand was on her throat then, pushing her head back so brutally that Laurie gazed up at him with terrified eyes. His mouth came down hard on hers, punishing her, forcing her lips open, his teeth grinding against hers, as the hand moved downward to rip open the bodice of her dress and clamp fiercely on her exposed breast.

Sickeningly, she felt her traitorous body begin to respond to his touch, and when, crushing her against his hard body, his mouth came down to pull greedily at a taut nipple, she groaned aloud.

Then his head came up and she felt the rough bristly cheek against hers, heard his voice rasping harshly in her ear.

'You still want me, Laurie. You know you do. Admit it.'

Then, just as she knew she could not withstand him or her own flaming desire for another second, she heard Jamie's voice again, a little more petulant this time. In a moment, she knew, he would start crying for her.

'No!' she cried, tearing herself from Miles' grasp and clutching her torn dress together to cover herself. 'No. It's too late. I want you to leave now and not come back. It's too late!'

Sobbing, she ran from him to the house and through the open door, slamming it shut behind her, shooting the bolt. As she raced up the stairs, she fought for control, her one thought to get to Jamie before his cries alerted Miles to his existence.

Willing herself to be calm, she went into the nursery and picked up the whimpering child. As she did so, she glanced out of the window, terrified that Miles would be at the door. He would be so furious by now, she thought, that he was perfectly capable of beating the door down.

When she saw his tall form striding purposefully down the hill, his broad shoulders set in anger, she heaved a sigh of relief, but as the bitter tears began to fall, she knew that underlying that relief was a sense of loss, of desolation, deeper and more profound than anything she had ever felt before.

\*    \*    \*

Laurie moved in a daze through the rest of the afternoon, her mind in a turmoil. What in the world was she going to do? At all costs she had to keep any knowledge of Jamie's existence from Miles.

She tired to reason it out. If he did find out she had had his child, what might he do about it? With all his power and influence he might try to take Jamie from her, to give him to Diana to raise. He'd said they weren't married yet, but that only meant they had probably postponed the wedding again.

But what if they had broken their engagement altogether? He'd said he'd been searching for her. Did that mean he wanted her and not Diana? Darcd she hope that if he had broken with Diana and knew Laurie had had his child he would want them both?

She snorted softly to herself in the darkness. That was only an idle daydream, a fantasy. Miles had never made her any promises except that he'd come back. And he did. He had never said he loved her, not once, not even when she had so gullibly and trustingly declared her love for him all those months ago.

No, she reasoned, her mind clear at last, the most she could ever hope for was that he would marry her out of a sense of duty. Shc knew he was a man who honoured his responsibilities. And he wanted her. He desired her. She knew that, too, from the way he had held her, looked at her, kissed her.

She groaned aloud, remembering. How long would desire last in the cold reality of everyday life, of raising a child? Without love on both sides to bind them, without deep emotional commitment, they would grow to hate and resent each other.

Besides, she thought with a sigh, such speculations were purely academic now. From the way she had treated him this afternoon and the way he had stalked off down the hill, she doubted if she would ever see him again anyway.

# CHAPTER EIGHT

THAT night after she had settled Jamie in his crib, Laurie decided to take a short walk down on the beach. Ever since Miles had left that afternoon, she had felt restless and jumpy. She knew Jamie would be safe. Once he was down for the night, he never budged until morning, and she would keep the house in sight.

She hesitated when she reached the beach, wondering whether to go right or left. The tide was out. It was a warm, balmy evening. She slipped off her sandals and walked towards the edge of the gently lapping surf.

Out of the corner of her eye she saw someone walking up the beach towards her, and she knew, without turning and looking, that it was Miles.

There was a slight breeze, warm on the evening air, lifting the hem of her skirt about her knees. She stood motionless, the waves curling about her bare feet, her sandals in her hand, waiting.

Then he was there beside her.

'We've got to talk,' she heard him say in a weary voice.

She turned to face him, her grey eyes wide and shining in the moonlight, her face grave. She watched as the breeze ruffled his thick hair. His hands were in his trousers pockets, his dark eyes brooding.

'I'm sorry I was so shrewish this afternoon,' she said in a stiff voice. 'I had no right . . .'

His fingers dug into her shoulders, then, startling her, cutting off her words. 'Damn it,' he growled, 'you had every right.' He sighed and dropped his hands to his sides. 'Let's go sit down,' he said, pointing to an outcropping of flat rock about ten feet from the shore.

They sat in silence for several moments, each absorbed in their own thoughts, close, but not touching. Still, Laurie was aware of the warmth of his body next to hers, and his unsteady breathing. Miles had lit a cigarette and sat smoking, not speaking, gazing out across the sea.

'I should have told you about Diana,' he said at last in a low voice. 'Somehow you seemed so remote up here on Cadranelle, so untouched by the world as I knew it, that I wanted to keep you separate from it, to . . .' He ground out his cigarette viciously against the rock. 'Hell, I don't know what I wanted. I only knew I had to get away, to sort it all out.'

Laurie searched for the words to say what was in her heart. She knew that whatever she said to him now would have far-reaching consequences and that she had to be very careful, both in what she told him and how she said it.

While it definitely did not seem the time or place to tell him about Jamie, still she could hardly question him about his feelings, his motive in seeking her out, with such a secret in her heart.

'It was such a shock,' she said at last, 'to find out you were engaged, especially when I hadn't heard a word from you for so many months.'

'But I *couldn't* get word to you,' he said. 'I was locked up in that damned house in Beirut.'

'I know that now, Miles.' She took a deep breath. 'I also know that you didn't force yourself on me when you were here with me.' She turned and smiled sadly at him, her face barely discernible in the pale moonlight. 'If anything, I did the forcing.'

He drew in his breath sharply. 'Don't look at me like that,' he said in a rasping voice. He raised a hand as if to touch her, then dropped it. 'I'd better tell you about Diana.'

Laurie's heart began to pound wildly in anticipation. Everything hinged on this. If he still intended to marry Diana, then she would just have to let him go. If not, then she would tell him about Jamie.

He began speaking in a low firm voice. 'Diana's father and my father were close friends. Mr Winthrop was the bank's lawyer. We always got along well, Diana and I. We had a lot in common. I told you when I was here before that it was time I settled down, that I wanted a family eventually, before I was forty.'

He paused. Laurie glanced at him out of the corner of her eye. He was staring into space, his jaw set, his mouth firm. 'I've had my share of romantic encounters,' he went on steadily. 'Travelling the way I do, the people I meet, brings me in contact with all kinds of people. I was tired of meaningless affairs. I'd never been really, wholeheartedly in love. Diana was there, waiting. I was fond of her. I thought we could have a good life together. We got engaged.'

He turned to her and the force of his will seemed to pull her around to face him. 'Then I met you,' he said softly, 'and I knew I could never settle for anything less than what we had.'

Laurie's heart soared. It was all she could do to keep from reaching out to him, putting her arms around him, drawing the dear head down to lie on her breast. She shivered.

'Are you cold?' asked Miles with concern. She shook her head.

He looked away again, and went on speaking. 'But you were so young. And I had to leave right away. I expected to be back in a few weeks, and in the meantime I would have a chance to think things through, to decide what to do—about you, about Diana. There wasn't time to talk to her before I left. Then,' he shrugged and spread his hands. 'I got stuck over there, and when I came back you'd disappeared.'

Laurie knew she had no right, but she had to ask. 'And what did you decide while you were gone?'

He ran a hand through his hair. Then he turned and looked at her. He was smiling crookedly.

'That I couldn't marry Diana, for one thing,' he replied. 'Not after I'd met you.'

Laurie had never known such sheer joy. She wanted to cry out with happiness and relief. He wasn't going to marry Diana. It would be all right.

Now, she thought, now was the time to tell him. She put a hand on his arm, thrilling to the touch of the hard muscles, the soft fine hairs covering his warm skin.

'Miles,' she began, 'there's something I've got to tell you.'

But he cut her off. 'No,' he said, 'I'm not finished.' He paused, then went on. 'The first thing I did was tell Diana I couldn't marry her. I wanted that settled before I came back here. Then, of course, you'd gone away. I didn't know what to think.'

'Miles, I can explain that, why I disappeared.'

'Oh, I know now. It was because you found out about Diana. I think I knew that all along. Then, when I saw you today, I was so relieved—and felt so guilty—that I barged in and half raped you.'

He stood up and reached out a hand and pulled her up beside him. Still holding her hand, he looked down at her gravely. 'I'm sorry about that. Can you forgive me?'

'Oh, Miles,' she cried, 'of course!' She longed to go to him, to feel his arms around her, but something in his expression, an indefinable coldness, held her back.

'I think we should get to know each other better,' he said. 'I've arranged for a leave from the bank. I don't have to work at all if I don't want to. I was a clumsy fool to rush you the way I did. Let's just be friends for a while and see where it leads.'

Laurie could only stare at him. What did that mean? Friends? How could they be 'friends' after what had passed between them? Didn't he want her, desire her, as she wanted and desired him? As she loved him. Not a word had passed his lips about love, about marriage, their future together. How could she tell him now, a virtual stranger, about his child? He would think she was trying to pressure him into a commitment he wasn't ready for.

Something of her dismay must have been visible, because his distant tone softened a little. He raised her hand to his mouth and softly kissed it, first each finger, then the palm. He looked down at her, his eyes gleaming.

'I think you know where I hope it leads,' he said, 'but let's not rush things.'

'No,' she murmured. 'Let's not do that.' Apparently the irony in her tone was lost on him, because he smiled and kissed her lightly on the mouth.

'I'll leave you now,' he said, 'but not for long.'

He turned and walked away from her. Laurie could only stare after him in despair. Did he want her, or didn't he? Was he just being noble because she was so young? She almost cried aloud in frustration as she trudged up the hill to the house, to Jamie.

Early the next morning, Emma appeared at the front door. She had taken to popping in at odd times on some flimsy excuse or other, but she and Laurie both knew it was to see Jamie.

'Well,' said Laurie with an indulgent smile as she opened the door to her, 'what is it this time? Did you bake too many cookies? Or an extra pie? Come on, out with it!'

Sheepishly, Emma held out a jar of raspberry jam.

'It's uncooked,' she mumbled, 'and won't keep. I guess I made too much.'

'Come on in.' Laurie heaved a mock sigh and took the jam. 'His Royal Highness is at breakfast.' They walked upstairs together to the kitchen. 'If you ask nicely, I may let you do the honours, but be prepared to get cereal and mashed banana all over you. He's taken to throwing his food—likes the gushy feel in his hands.'

The two women sat at the kitchen table drinking coffee while Emma happily fed Jamie in his high chair, blissfully unconcerned about the dabs of food that ended up on the apron Laurie had insisted she wear.

'You see what I mean,' Laurie remarked dryly as Emma wiped a handful of cereal from her plump cheek.

'Don't even listen to her, Jamie,' said Emma to the delighted baby, 'you're perfect just the way you are.'

'I'm sure he'd agree with you,' Laurie said. 'He's a man, isn't he?'

Emma shot her a sharp look. Laurie flushed and lowered her eyes.

'I'm sorry,' she muttered. 'That was a stupid thing to say.'

Silently, Emma cleaned Jamie's face and hands and wiped off the tray of the high chair, then she lifted him up and put him in his play pen, where he happily began pulling a battered rag doll apart.

'All right,' said Emma, as she sat back down across from Laurie, 'what's wrong?'

'Nothing's wrong.'

'Don't give me that.' There was a short silence, while Emma seemed to be debating within herself. Then, 'He's back, isn't he?'

'Who's back?'

Emma rolled her eyes in silent supplication. 'Miles Cutler, that's who. I saw his boat down at the dock yesterday, and I knew he'd make a beeline straight here. What happened?'

Laurie shifted uncomfortably in her chair. 'Nothing happened, Em. I don't want to talk about it.'

Emma sighed. 'You're not making sense. If nothing happened, why don't you want to talk about it?' She hesitated. 'Did he bring his wife?'

Laurie got up and went to the stove to refill her coffee cup. She stood there a long time, her arms braced rigidly on the edge of the counter, her back to Emma. Except for the ticking of the clock and Jamie's happy gurgling, the room was silent.

Finally she turned around, her face white and pinched.

'He's not married,' she said dully. 'He wasn't married when I knew him before. I just assumed . . . He was engaged.'

Emma thought this over. 'I see.' There was sympathy in her eyes. 'Still, he should take some responsibility for Jamie. He has money, position.

His fiancée will just have to accept that.'

'He's not even engaged any more.'

Emma's eyes widened. 'Well then, what's the problem? Wouldn't he accept the baby?' she asked gently.

'I didn't tell him.'

Emma's eyes flew open wider and her cup clattered on to the saucer. 'You didn't tell him? Why ever not, for heaven's sake?'

Laurie sat back down at the table and gazed across at Emma with troubled eyes.

'I just couldn't,' she said. 'I don't know how he feels about me after all this time. We knew each other for such a little while. What purpose would it serve to tell him? I don't want him to marry me out of a sense of duty. He'd only grow to hate me.'

Emma put a hand over Laurie's. 'But, my dear, he has a right to know. It's his child, too.'

Laurie gave her a stricken look. 'You really think I should tell him?'

'I really do,' Emma replied solemnly.

'Oh, Em, I don't know if I can.'

Emma gave her hand a little pat and stood up. 'Why don't you go for a little walk? I'll just clean up the kitchen and get Master James settled for his morning nap. The fresh air will do you good. You might even feel like going down towards the harbour. Lots of interesting sights there.'

A few minutes later Laurie found herself walking up the path to the road that led to the boat dock. Even though it was a sunny day, hot and dry, she

found herself shivering uncontrollably. She could
hear the seed pods of the yellow broom cracking
open in the heavy stillness, and the soft chirp of the
grasshoppers in the shrubbery by the side of the
road.

She knew Emma was right: Miles did have a right
to know about Jamie. But every instinct within her
rebelled against his pity, his sense of duty. She
would just have to make it clear to him, she
decided, that she wanted nothing from him. If he
wanted, he could come to see Jamie, even have him
for visits when he was older.

She was at the top of the hill, now, looking down
at the busy harbour below. Her eyes scanned the
long line of boats tied up on both sides of the
wooden dock. There was no sign of Miles' boat.

Slowly she started down the steep incline. She
saw Carl walking towards her on his morning
rounds, collecting moorage fees, and headed
straight for him.

'Good morning, Carl.'

He glanced up at her, his pipe in his mouth.
'Morning, Laurie. Beautiful day.'

'Carl,' she said when she reached his side, 'have
you seen Miles Cutler's boat this morning?'

He gave her a blank look. 'What's its name?'

'I don't know. It's that big custom-built Chris
Craft, about sixty feet.'

Carl reached under his cap with his good arm and
scratched his head. 'Let's see. Out of Seattle, as I
remember.' Then the light dawned. 'I know. Big
boat for one man to handle.'

'Where is it, Carl?' she asked, trying to hide her impatience.

'Oh, he left.' Laurie's heart sank. 'Paid for a week, though, so maybe he plans to come back.'

'If he does come back and you see him, Carl, would you tell him I must talk to him? He knows where I live.'

Carl cocked his head to one side and gave her a quizzical look. 'Okay,' he said finally. 'If I see him.'

'Thanks, Carl.' She turned to go.

He called after her, 'Have you seen Emma this morning?'

'Yes, she's at the house taking care of Jamie.'

Carl grunted. 'Mighta known,' he said, and went back to his rounds.

After Emma had gone home, Laurie fidgeted away the rest of the morning, moving restlessly from room to room, doing unnecessary jobs, jumping at every noise thinking it might be Miles coming back. Now that she had made up her mind to tell him about Jamie, she was anxious to get it over with.

She fed the baby at noon and toyed with her own lunch while he played on the blanket at her feet, trying to propel himself forward on his stomach. He would be crawling soon, and she'd have to get a gate to put across the stairs.

She put him down for his afternoon nap at two o'clock and decided she'd go mad with waiting if she didn't find something constructive to do. She set up her easel out in the clearing at the back of the house and forced herself to concentrate on her work. After a time, she became totally absorbed in it and succeeded in putting Miles out of her mind at last.

After an hour or so of steady work, she set her brush down and stretched to get the kinks out of her shoulder muscles. Her new technique seemed to be working quite well.

She looked up to see Ted walking towards her. 'Ted,' she called, 'what are you doing here? I thought you'd gone to Neah Bay fishing.'

He gave her a disgusted look. 'We did, but the place is crawling with tourists. If there were any fish there to begin with, the darned boaters scared them all off.'

He sat down on a garden chair and slumped dejectedly.

'I'm sorry, Ted.' Laurie giggled and he gave her a sharp look. 'What's so funny?' he demanded.

'Oh, I don't know,' she replied, struggling to keep a straight face, 'you just look so . . . so . . .' She started laughing again.

Finally, in spite of himself, he had to join in. 'It was pretty funny,' he admitted at last, 'to see all the fishermen up on their decks shouting and waving their fists.'

'And, of course, the tourists didn't pay any attention to you.'

'Hell, no,' he exploded. 'They'd just whizz by on their damned water skis and laugh at us.' He shook his head disgustedly.

They sat together in a companionable silence for some time. It was so peaceful, Laurie thought, so quiet and safe here. She dreaded the thought of disturbing her hard-earned tranquillity with the unpleasant task she had ahead of her.

'Why don't you go in and make us some iced tea?' she suggested after a while. 'I just have one more little place here to finish up, then I'm going to quit for the day.'

'Okay.' Ted rose to his feet, then looked down at her hesitantly. 'Er—how's the screamer been?'

She hid a smile. 'Top of his form. Only he's not really screaming much these days. He appears to be quite satisfied with his lot in life.'

He gave her an appreciative look. 'And well he should be, with a mother like you.' He grunted, and turned to go. 'I'll just go in and make the tea.'

'Right. You know where everything is.'

Laurie returned to her painting. The light would be gone soon and she had one more little detail she wanted to correct while Ted made the iced tea.

He hadn't been gone five minutes when she heard someone call her name.

'Hello, Laurie.' It was Miles.

He was walking towards her, and she drew in her breath sharply at the sight of him. He was wearing blue denim trousers, belted and slung low on his narrow hips, and his long, powerfully muscled legs strained against them as he strode across the clearing easily and lithely. A lightweight knit shirt covered his chest and shoulders.

'Hello, Miles.' He was beside her now, looking down at the painting on the easel.

'That's very good,' he commented. 'You've changed your style.' He turned to face her. 'Carl Bendiksen said you wanted to see me.'

'Yes,' she murmured. Now that he was here, so tall, so remote and forbidding, she didn't know how to begin. Should she just blurt it out? Or work up to it in a roundabout way? He seemed determined to keep a distance between them. He stood there like a stranger, waiting for her to speak.

She looked up at him. His face was serious, but his eyes were kind. I love him so much, she thought, and to her dismay she could feel tears stinging her eyes.

He made a low sound deep in his throat and reached down for her, pulling her up out of her chair to hold her to him, his strong arms around her now, stroking her back, her face, her hair.

This was where she belonged, she thought, carried away on a wave of pure bliss. Her tears now were tears of joy. His caress was gentle, reassuring, and he murmured low in her ear as his hands soothed away all the pain.

'Laurie, Laurie, darling, don't. It's all right. Everything will be all right. I'm here now. I won't leave you ever again.'

'Oh, Miles,' she whispered, flinging her arms around his neck, 'I've missed you so!'

He held her face between his hands and looked down at her. 'God,' he breathed, 'I was so worried about you! I was about ready to hire detectives, but then I decided your disappearance must have been deliberate, that you hated me for what I'd done to you.' His arms went around her again. 'It was a torment to me, wanting to explain, not being able to find you.'

He kissed her, gently, lovingly, her hair, her eyes, her cheeks, light kisses that lingered on her skin like tongues of fire. Then his lips were on hers, sweet and tender.

Locked in his gentle embrace, Laurie forgot everything, all the hurt of the past months, all the pain and remorse when she had thought she had lost him. She was swept away on a tide of longing for the strong man who held her.

His lips were at her ear now, his face buried in the silky black hair, his hands moving possessively over her back.

'You can forget what I said last night about wanting to be friends,' he growled. 'I don't know what I could have been thinking of. I wanted . . .' He broke off. 'You're so young. But I want you now. I don't want to wait. I can't wait.'

Miles still wants me, Laurie thought, and it seemed as though her heart would leap out of her body. Miles still wants me. Everything was going to be all right.

Her arms tightened around his neck, her hands clutched at the thick hair growing there and she arched her body closer to him.

He drew in a sharp breath, and then his mouth was on hers again, hard and demanding this time. She parted her lips with a little moan of joy.

His hands came up under her thin blouse,

roaming wildly over her bare back, then around in front to clasp her breasts, moving from one to the other in demanding possession.

Then, just as he started to unbutton her blouse, she heard it, the little gurgling sounds that meant Jamie was awake. Her whole body stiffened in shock. Jamie! She had forgotten all about him. And Ted! Had he seen?

She didn't care. She'd never lied to Ted. All she could think of was that she had to tell Miles now, immediately, about his son.

'What is it, darling?' asked Miles, tearing his lips from hers and giving her a searching look. 'What's wrong?'

'Miles,' she said, 'there's something I've got to tell you, something you don't know about. I tried to tell you last night, but . . .'

Then she heard Ted's voice coming from the porch, where he was hidden from view.

'Laurie,' he called to her, 'I think Jamie might be catching a cold. He's got a sniffle and sneezed twice. What kind of mother are you . . .'

His voice broke off as he stepped off the porch and came around to take in the sight of Miles and Laurie standing together. At the first sound of Ted's voice, she had jumped back, out of Miles' arms. She gazed past him now in horror as she saw Ted standing there holding Jamie in his arms, a puzzled look on his face.

Miles whirled around. The two men glared at each other, and Laurie could see recognition dawning in Ted's brown eyes.

'Take your hands off her, you bastard,' he muttered in a low, menacing voice.

With a little cry, Laurie stumbled over to him and grasped Jamie from him.

'No, Ted,' she pleaded, 'please, no!'

He didn't even glance at her. His eyes were riveted on the tall dark man he had recognised from the sketches Laurie had made of him.

'Miles . . .' she called as she took a step towards him. The look of cold fury he threw at her made her stop in her tracks. 'Please, Miles,' she whispered, shaken by the look of contempt in the blue-green eyes. 'It's not what you think.'

His eyes flicked at her. His lips curled in a cruel line. 'How do you know what I think, Laurie?' His voice was hard with barely-controlled fury, his fists clenched at his sides. 'All I know is what I see. Are you this child's mother?'

'Yes, but you don't understand . . .' she wailed. Jamie had started to cry by now, and she could barely make herself heard over his frightened screams.

Then, as she watched in horror, she saw Ted cross the few feet that separated him from Miles and raise his fist.

'I'll kill you!' he shouted.

Miles, taller and stronger, parried the blow neatly and pulled Ted's arm around, clamping it firmly against his back.

'I wouldn't try anything, sonny,' Miles bit out. 'I could flatten you without trying.'

Ted, struggling wildly, furiously, managed to

free himself from that iron grip and turned to strike again.

'You asked for it,' said Miles on a note of triumph, and with a powerful sudden stroke, his fist met Ted's jaw and laid him out on his back.

Stunned, Ted raised himself up on one elbow. He put a hand to his jaw and shook his head. A little trickle of blood appeared at the corner of his mouth.

Miles stood over him, a cold, self-satisfied, mirthless smile on his face.

'I warned you,' he said pleasantly. His glance flicked to the stunned and horrified Laurie, still trying to comfort Jamie, whose screams had quietened into injured sobbing. 'Believe me,' Miles went on, glancing down at Ted, 'she's not worth fighting over.'

He turned and stalked off. Laurie was torn between the frantic desire to run after him and the need to stay and look after Ted. She made up her mind then. She couldn't let Miles go. She called to him as she ran towards his retreating figure.

'Miles, please believe me,' she cried after him. 'It's not what you think. Please let me explain!'

But Jamie had started screaming again, and either Miles didn't—or wouldn't—hear her. At any rate, he never looked back, and as she stood helplessly at the top of the rise trying at the same time to comfort the sobbing child and choke back her own tears, she saw him disappear from view.

# CHAPTER NINE

LATER, Laurie had her hands full quieting Jamie and tending to Ted. She had set Jamie in his high chair with a squishy overripe banana to play with, beyond caring what kind of mess he made now. She had helped Ted into her father's surgery and bathed his face. He wasn't badly hurt, merely stunned, with only a cut on his lip to account for all the blood.

All the while she was working over him, he kept his eyes averted from her and only replied to her brief questions about how he felt and where it hurt with curt monosyllables. She knew he was both angry with her and ashamed of the beating he'd taken, so she didn't press him.

Finally, when he was cleaned up and seemed to have recovered from the blow, she left him, still a little groggy, to run upstairs and see to Jamie.

She had tied him securely in his chair and found him happily squishing banana in his tiny hands. As she cleaned him up and fed him his dinner, her one thought was to get to Miles, to explain to him before it was too late.

She knew how it must have looked and didn't blame him for jumping to the conclusion he had obviously come to. What else could he think when he saw Ted coming out of her house with such a proprietorial air, holding what Miles must have assumed was Ted's child, referring to her as its mother.

When she had settled Jamie into his playpen, she ran back downstairs to see how Ted was getting along. He was standing at the bottom of the stairs, a hangdog look on his face.

'Well, I really protected your honour today, didn't I, Laurie?' he croaked through puffy lips.

'Oh, Ted,' she sighed, putting a hand on his arm. 'Please don't.'

He flinched away from her touch and sighed. 'Not that your honour needs protecting,' he added in a bitter tone.

She stiffened. 'What do you mean by that?'

'Well, it's obvious, isn't it?' he asked, shrugging. 'You still love him, don't you? I saw the way you looked at him, the way he was holding you, how you ran after him.'

She looked away. She didn't know what to say, how to answer him.

'Yes,' she said at last in a small voice. 'Yes, I do. I always have. I always will.'

'That just about says it all, then. Don't feel bad on my account, Laurie,' he said as he saw her stricken look. 'You never lied to me.' They were silent for a moment. 'Well, I'll be going now,' he said gruffly. 'We're going up to the Yuclataws tomorrow. Not so many tourists that far north.' Then he was gone.

\*     \*     \*

Laurie knew what she had to do now. She ran upstairs to comb her hair and wash her face. She changed from the pants and shirt, spotted and crumpled now from the afternoon's exertions, into her blue shirtwaist dress.

She glanced in the mirror for a final survey. Her eyes were over-bright from all the shocks she had received today and with the anticipation of seeing Miles again, but she would have to do.

Quickly, before she could change her mind, she gathered up the heavy-eyed Jamie and put some clean clothes for him in a plastic sack. She just wanted to keep moving, get on with what she had to do. It would be so easy now to give up, to take the coward's way out and crawl back in her shell, but she knew she had to confront Miles, had to make him understand.

What if he didn't believe her? she worried as she locked the cottage door behind her and started up the hill to the hotel. She would *make* him believe her, she vowed fiercely. At least she had to try.

Emma was in the kitchen cleaning up after supper, perspiration streaming down her plump red face. When she saw Laurie come in, carrying Jamie, her face lit up and she reached out for him.

'Oh, my aching feet!' she moaned, sinking into a chair. 'Thank goodness it's almost Labor Day. I don't think I could stand another week of tourists!'

Laurie hesitated. 'Em, I was going to ask you to keep Jamie for me overnight, but if you're too tired . . .'

'Too tired?' Emma exclaimed indignantly. 'For

Jamie? You must be joking! The tourists can go whistle for all I care.' She cuddled the sleeping baby to her ample bosom, then gave Laurie a sharp look, taking in the girl's glittering eyes and tense posture.

'What's wrong?'

'I'll explain later. It's a long story. Now I've got to go.'

Emma nodded, then watched Laurie leave with troubled eyes and a deep sigh.

Laurie willed herself not to run up the paved road and down to the boat dock. The sun was just setting and people were straggling back down to their boats before dark, exhausted from another strenuous vacation day.

As she started down the hill to the harbour she hardly dared look to see if Miles' boat was still there, but at last she began to scan to long wharf as she came closer.

He was gone. She took one more look, then slowly turned and started back up the hill.

The weeks passed slowly. After Labor Day, the last straggling tourist had left regretfully to back to the city, and life on Cadranelle settled down into a normal routine.

It was late September. Miles had been gone a month, and with each passing day Laurie had to steel herself anew to the fact that she had lost him, would probably never see him again. Every evening, just before sunset, she would walk down to the harbour with Jamie in her arms to see if his boat might be there, but it never was.

When Laurie had finally told Emma what had happened at that last terrible meeting, Emma had tried to convince her that she should go to him in Seattle, or at least call. Laurie dreaded the thought of putting any kind of pressure on him, and the look of contempt on his face that day when he had seen Ted with Jamie still haunted her. She tormented herself for weeks debating the issue.

Finally, one dreary wet afternoon, after she had settled Jamie for his nap, she gave in and dialled Miles' office number. If he wouldn't talk to her, or was cold and rejecting, at least she would have tried.

'Business Extension Department, Mr Cutler's office,' came the crisp voice of Margaret Ferrar over the telephone.

'May I speak to Mr Cutler, please?' Laurie asked politely.

'I'm sorry, Mr Cutler is on an extended leave. Would you care to leave your name and number? He does call in occasionally for messages.'

'When do you expect him back?'

'I really don't know. He left in July and said he might be gone several months.'

'Thank you,' said Laurie flatly. She gave Mrs Ferrar her name and number and hung up.

That night there was a party at the hotel, a farewell dinner for the fishermen who were leaving the next day for Alaska. Laurie put in a token appearance, but her heart wasn't in the festivities.

Aside from helping Emma serve and clean up, she sat in the background holding Jamie on her lap.

He was growing into a strapping, husky baby, three months old now, and each day Laurie noticed the grey eyes turning almost imperceptibly into the same deep blue-green as his father's, a constant reminder of the man she loved and could never have.

Emma came and sat down beside her, wiping her hands on her apron. 'Well,' she said with a sigh, 'the men will be leaving tomorrow.'

Laurie didn't answer. She was watching the roomful of people. Someone had turned on a record player and several were dancing. She saw Ted touch Debbie lightly on the arm, saw the blonde girl's face light up as she turned into his arms.

Laurie smiled and turned to Emma. 'I think your Debbie is finding that Cadranelle isn't so dull after all.'

Emma had seen, too. 'You don't mind?' she asked, giving Laurie a searching look.

'Mind? Why should I mind?' Laurie was puzzled. 'I think it's great. Don't you? Ted's a fine boy.'

'Hardly a boy,' Emma answered dryly. 'He's a man, in case you hadn't noticed.'

Laurie laughed. 'I guess you're right. I just always think of him that way. I guess I just compare him to . . .' She broke off in confusion.

Emma cleared her throat. 'Well, of course, I'm delighted,' she hastened on. 'About Ted and

Debbie, that is. I was just afraid . . . I mean, I
thought you and Ted . . .'

Laurie shook her head. 'No. I love Ted, but not
the way he deserves to be loved. He always knew
that.'

They sat in silence, watching the dancers, listening to the music, thinking their own thoughts.

At last Emma spoke. 'It's still him, isn't it,
Laurie?' she asked gently. 'Miles Cutler.'

Laurie smiled sadly and pressed Emma's hand.
She nodded. 'I'm afraid so. It always will be.'

'Isn't there anything you can do? Anything I can
do?'

Laurie shrugged. 'I can't think what. He's gone.
I've just got to learn to live with that fact.' She
glanced down at Jamie's drooping eyes and stood
up. 'I must go get this young man to bed.'

Emma walked with her to the door. 'Come up for
coffee tomorrow. I hardly ever see you any more.'

Laurie smiled without replying and waved as she
walked down the steps. 'I'll see. I've been pretty
busy.'

'Laurie!' There was a harsh note in Emma's voice
that made Laurie turn around swiftly. 'Laurie.' Her
voice was softer now. 'You've got to snap out of it,
you know. You can't grieve for ever.'

Laurie swallowed hard and nodded. 'I know,
Em. I know.'

That night in bed Laurie thought about what Emma
had said. She knew she was right. She had vir-
tually abandoned her painting, neglected her

appearance, and aside from taking care of Jamie and performing the minimum household chores, she spent most of her time moping, trying to read, taking long aimless walks.

The next morning was bright and warm, and Laurie got up with a renewed sense of vigour. She would turn over a new leaf, she promised herself, and try to get on with her life again.

At first, it was a struggle just to get herself going, to focus her mind on the tasks at hand and close it to brooding thoughts of a past that could not be altered. She had become so used to her lethargic way of life that it took all her will-power to do the simplest task.

She decided to start with the house. It hadn't had a thorough cleaning since she had left in the spring to go to Seattle. At breakfast she made a list of each task that needed doing, in order of priority, and determined to stick with it until it was all done and the house was spotless and shining again.

She started with the kitchen, scrubbing out the stove and refrigerator, emptying the cupboards and washing down the insides, discarding old containers of food. Then she scoured the floor on her hands and knees, rinsed it, and when it was dry, waxed it to shiny perfection.

It was noon by then, time to feed Jamie and fix her own lunch. Laurie was tired; it had been an exhausting morning. But as she settled Jamie into his high chair and tied a fresh bib around his neck, the gleaming kitchen gave her a sense of accomplishment and deep satisfaction.

As she fed the baby, spooning strained vegetables into the eager mouth, his solemn eyes riveted on her as he ate with relish, she was struck with how strongly he was beginning to resemble Miles. The light baby fuzz on his head was turning darker, growing thicker every day, and the bone structure under the baby fat was identical. But it was the eyes that were the most startling, the same deep blue-green as his father's, the colour of the sea.

She reached down impulsively to give him a quick kiss on the cheek. As she did so, he turned his head to see what was happening to the source of his food, and Laurie got some of the strained peas on her face.

She laughed out loud, and as she reached for a napkin to wipe the mess off her face, she stopped short, the hand still in mid-air, as she realised that was the first time she had laughed—really laughed—since Miles had left.


That afternoon she got out her sketchbook and made some quick studies of Jamie in various attitudes and poses. She wished now she hadn't torn up and burned the ones she had done of Miles, but it was probably just as well. She had to forget, and those revealing sketches would have been a constant painful reminder.

She didn't feel quite ready yet to tackle her seascapes. She would have all winter to work on those, anyway. They had sold very well this summer, and she had enough money now at least until next tourist season.

That evening, after her usual light supper, she decided it was time to break the habit she had formed of walking down to the harbour before dark. It had become an exercise in futility anyway. She was beginning to accept the fact that Miles was not coming back, ever. It only made it harder for her if she clung to false hopes.

The next few days were cool and drizzly. Laurie kept faithfully to her house-cleaning schedule, crossing off each task as it was accomplished, and by Friday, all that was left to do was the windows.

Luckily, the day dawned bright and clear, one of those rare sultry days in early fall that left her panting and perspiring with her exertions by noon. The air was heavy and still. Not a bird sang. The sea looked flat and oily, placid and unmoving, without a breath of a breeze to disturb the calm blue surface. Even with all the windows open, the house was too warm.

After lunch, Laurie decided to go down to the sea for a swim. She had a small portable canvas bed for Jamie that collapsed into a compact, lightweight package, so he could nap on the beach while she swam.

She put on her old one-piece bathing suit and a light cotton beach robe, gathered up Jamie and his bed and set off down the hill. It wasn't until she got there that Laurie realised there was no safe place to set up the portable bed where Jamie would be protected from the glaring sun. She looked around at the flat expanse of rock and sand, sighed, and gave him a rueful smile.

'You know, young man, you're getting to be a problem.'

He wiggled and grinned up at her, clutching at her hair as she bent over him, tangling it in his tiny fists. She kissed him lightly on the forehead, the baby skin soft as a flower petal under her lips, and hugged him close.

As she started back up the hill, ruefully abandoning her visions of a cool swim, it suddenly occurred to her that there was plenty of shade at the small lake. It was surrounded by enormous trees and heavy shrubbery. It was only a quarter of a mile away, not too far to carry Jamie and the bed.

By the time she reached the lake, however, she regretted her decision. Little rivulets of perspiration coursed down her face, her back, between her breasts, and mingled with the dust from the walk on the dirt path to form a sticky, grimy coating on her skin that was decidedly unpleasant. Her feet in their sandals were covered with dirt.

She stood at the edge of the lake, debating whether to turn back and forget it, but the clear blue water looked so inviting, she decided to take one quick dip to wash the grime off before she went back home. Besides, Jamie was fast asleep by now, and she might as well take advantage of that.

She laid him down on the grassy knoll that led down to the lakeshore while she set up the canvas bed. She placed it in the shade of a madrona tree, then put him gently in the bed, watching him for a few seconds to make sure he was fast asleep. She covered him loosely with mosquito netting against the insects, then shed her robe, slipped off her sandals, and ran down the grass slope.

She glided smoothly into the cool water and swam for fifteen minutes or so, never venturing far in case Jamie cried out. The water felt delicious, just the right temperature, and when she climbed out she felt clean and refreshed.

Jamie was still sleeping soundly. It would be a shame to wake him now, she thought. She spread out her robe on the grass and lay down for a while in the sun. After half an hour of baking, she began to feel uncomfortably warm again and decided to take one more dip before starting out on the dusty walk home.

Her bathing suit had dried by now, however, and she hated to get it wet again. She debated for a moment, a daring thought forming in her mind. No one would be coming to the lake this time of year. The tourists were all gone, the men up fishing. What harm would it do? She had always wanted to try it.

She hesitated for just a fraction of a second, then quickly slipped off the bathing suit and ran lightly down to the water, dropping her robe at the very edge just in case someone did show up and she had to get out in a hurry.

The water felt heavenly against her bare skin. It was a sensation she had never experienced before, sensuous and liberating. She had never felt so free as she did now, her lithe slender body cutting through the near-transparent water, just like a golden fish.

Lost in the pleasure of the moment, she wasn't aware that she was being watched until a flicker of movement at the far end of the lake, a sudden glint in the sunshine, caught her eye.

She froze, her feet just touching bottom, and slowly turned her head in that direction. There, not a hundred feet away, stood a man, bare-chested, his deeply tanned chest and shoulders gleaming in the sunshine.

Laurie knew it was Miles even before she tossed her head to shake the water out of her eyes so that she could focus on his face. She knew that form, that arrogant, confident stance, so well. He stood there, legs apart, arms folded across his chest like some marauding pirate, watching her.

She flushed deeply under that penetrating gaze. Even though her whole body was submerged, the water was so clear that it was quite obvious she was naked. Still, she couldn't move. As their eyes locked together, her heart began to pound wildly. She couldn't think, could hardly breathe.

Then, before she knew what was happening, she saw Miles slip off his trousers to reveal dark bathing trunks, saw the strong tanned legs moving towards the water, and in what seemed like a split second, saw him swimming towards her with long powerful strokes.

By the time she had collected herself enough to turn in panic and head for shore, it was too late. She was trapped. She felt a muscular arm clamp around her throat, felt herself pulled back in the water against a bare chest.

She fought desperately to get free of that crushing grip, wriggling and twisting in his arms, digging her fingernails into his bare flesh, kicking at him, her wet slippery body sliding against his as she struggled.

Then she felt his hands come up to cup her breasts, his head come down so that his rough cheek was against hers, his lips at her ear.

'Don't fight me, Laurie,' he murmured. 'I won't hurt you.'

His hands moved possessively on her body down to her waist, across her stomach, back up to pass over her breasts again, and with a sigh, she let go and slumped back against him.

'That beautiful body,' he whispered in her ear as his hands moulded every curve.

He turned her around then to face him, and she looked up into those blinding eyes and knew she was lost again.

'Oh, Miles,' she whispered.

His arms were hard around her as he bent to cover her mouth with his. As her lips parted, she heard him groan, and his hands came down to her hips to pull her against him and his hard masculine need.

They were moving now, slowly and gracefully in the water, like partners in a dance, his strong thighs propelling her backwards until they reached the shore and she felt herself laid gently down on the grass, his body half covering hers.

His lips were on her breast now, and as his mouth closed on a thrusting nipple, she pulled the dark head closer into the soft fullness, straining her body towards him as his hands moved feverishly down to her thighs, parting her legs.

Just as he reached down to tug at the waistband of his bathing trunks, she heard the gurgling sound that meant Jamie was waking from his nap.

Immediately her head cleared, and she raised herself up on her elbows. Miles must have heard it, too, because his hands had stopped their frenzied exploration.

'It's the baby,' she said in a low voice. 'I must go to him.'

Without looking at her, he rolled to one side, freeing her. She jumped up, grabbed the robe that was lying nearby and slipped it on. When she checked on Jamie, he was smiling happily and staring intently at the patterns made by the madrona leaves above him gently bobbing in the slight breeze that had come up.

Her thoughts were in a turmoil. Why had Miles returned? What did it mean? Was it an accident that they had met like this and he would just vanish again? She thought of the pain of the last year and of her new sense of purpose, of hard-earned stability and acceptance of her loss. Would she have to retrace each painful step all over again?

No, she thought, as she turned back to him. I won't go through that again. I'll make one attempt to explain things to him, then say goodbye for good. She began walking towards him. He was on the grass where she had left him, standing now, tall and composed, staring out over the lake. She pulled her cotton robe tightly about her and shivered. This wasn't going to be easy.

'Miles,' she said in a firm voice.

At the sound, he turned his head swiftly. She couldn't read his expression. His face was controlled, his eyes narrowed.

'I know you're not married, Laurie,' he said at last. 'I checked.' He glanced down at her hand. 'You're not wearing a ring. You weren't before, either.'

'No, Miles, I'm not married.'

He made an impatient gesture with his hand, and for a second anger flashed in the hooded eyes.

'Well, what the hell's wrong with the guy that he won't marry you?' he barked. 'He seemed domestic enough that day at the house.' There was a sneering tone to his voice that made Laurie wince.

'It's not his child,' she said calmly. She had nothing to apologise for, she thought. He would not make her crawl.

His eyes widened in disbelief, then narrowed again as he met her steady gaze.

'My, you have been a busy girl,' he sneered mockingly. 'It seems I taught you a little too well!'

A little knot of anger at his tone, his bland assumption that somehow she was entirely to blame for an event that was at last partly his fault, began to flare up in the pit of Laurie's stomach. She clenched her fists at her sides.

'What lesson was that, Miles? Deception?' He

gave her a hard look and took a threatening step towards her, but she held her ground without flinching. 'Has it never occurred to you,' she went on in a strong voice, 'that it might be *your* child?'

She glared at him and with intense satisfaction saw that cold gaze falter.

'*My* child!' he repeated, obviously stunned. 'How could it be my child?'

'Can't you count?' she snapped. 'You were here the first of October, and Jamie was born in July. It still takes nine months, you know, even for superior beings like you.'

Miles was frowning now. He turned and walked away from her a few paces. She watched him for a long time, able to tell nothing from the broad back, the shoulders slightly slumped now. He seemed to be deep in thought.

Jamie started whimpering, and she ran to him, soothing him with low comforting sounds. He needed changing and would be hungry soon. Laurie gathered him up and went out to the grassy verge to set him down so she could pack up his bed.

Miles was staring thoughtfully at her as she approached with the baby in her arms. She could tell he wasn't convinced, and suddenly she knew what to do.

She walked straight towards him. When she stood before him, she held the baby out to him. 'Here,' she said, 'meet your son, Jamie. Please hold him for me while I pack up his bed.' He gave her a startled look. 'And while you're at it,' she went on in a firm voice, 'you might take a good look at his eyes. They're exactly the colour of yours—an unusual colour. Hardly a coincidence.'

Wordlessly, Miles reached out and took the baby from her. She turned and went back into the shadows of the trees, her knees shaking now in the aftermath of what she had done. Would he believe her at last?

# CHAPTER TEN

'OF course I'll marry you,' Miles said stiffly.

It was evening and they were back at the house. Laurie had fed Jamie and put him down for the night. Although it seemed Miles had accepted him as his son, even going so far as to carry him back from the lake, he handled him gingerly and seemed visibly relieved when she took him from him.

'Don't do me any favours,' Laurie snapped. She was working in the kitchen, putting together a scratch meal. Miles stood at the edge of the island counter, his hands in his trousers pockets. 'I've managed quite well on my own so far,' she added.

She slammed the oven door shut with a bang, burning her hand in the process, and sending a bowl of eggs crashing to the floor.

'Oh, damn,' she muttered as she stopped to clean up the mess.

'Laurie, listen to me.' His voice was gentle, pleading. She was at the sink, rinsing out the sticky bowl, and heard him come up behind her. She turned around.

'I'm listening.'

He sighed and ran a hand through his thick dark hair. Her heart yearned to reach out to him, to feel his arms around her, but she stood firm.

'You must understand,' he said at last, 'this has

all been a terrible shock to me. I only want to do what's best for everyone concerned. It just never occurred to me when I saw the three of you together that day looking so domestic that the baby didn't belong to what's-his-name.'

'Ted,' she said in a clear voice. 'His name is Ted. We grew up together. We've been like brother and sister. He's been a good friend, nothing more. He came to get me at the hospital after Jamie was born and grew fond of him. He's a very lovable baby.'

Miles winced at that and turned away. 'All right, then, Ted,' he said. Then he turned accusing eyes on her. 'Why didn't you tell me before?'

'I *tried* to tell you,' she cried out bitterly. 'When I first knew I was pregnant, my first thought was to go to you, but I didn't know where you were. Then when I found out what happened in Lebanon, and knew you'd come back, I flew, *that day*, the very day I read it in the newspaper, and ran right in to Diana Winthrop.'

Miles spread his hands in a helpless gesture. 'I explained about Diana.'

'Yes, I know about that now, but I didn't then. I'm trying to tell you why I did what I did.' She paused.

'All right, go on.' His voice was tight.

'Then when you came back and said you wanted to be *friends*,' she cried, 'how could I tell you? "Oh, by the way, *friend*, we have a child."'

'Laurie, I just didn't want to rush you into an intimate relationship before we'd gotten to know each other better. God, it had only been three days before. I wanted to give us a little time.'

'But I didn't have any time!' she cried.

She turned from him so he wouldn't see the tears that were threatening to spill over. She stood at the sink, her hands braced against the edge, struggling for control.

'Miles,' she said at last in a tight voice, 'why did you come back?'

He was silent for so long that she finally turned around, thinking he might have gone.

'I think you know why,' he said in a low voice full of meaning. 'I think I showed you why up at the lake this afternoon.' Laurie coloured deeply at the reminder of that passionate encounter and her wanton response to his kisses and caresses. 'I wanted you,' he went on in a weary voice. 'I checked the register at the county office in Friday Harbor after Margaret gave me the message that you'd called. I remembered you weren't wearing a ring. It's not my habit to interfere in marriages, but it seemed you were—might be—free.' He shrugged. 'I wanted you,' he said simply. 'I decided to give it a try.'

'And succeeded,' Laurie said bitterly. 'Almost.' He *wanted* her, she thought, while I'm so crazy in love with him I couldn't deny him anything.

He came up to her and put his hands on her shoulders, looking down into her eyes. She felt herself sinking, sinking under that steady gaze.

'You want me, too,' he said, forcing her head back when she tried to turn away. 'You know you do. And we have Jamie to think of. If we both try, we can forget the past and build a good life together.'

A life without love, Laurie thought sadly. But she knew he was right. They did have to think of Jamie. She knew he was marrying her out of a sense of duty, and that she had to agree to a loveless marriage for the same reason.

'All right,' she said at last. 'If it's what you want. I'll marry you.'

They were married quietly a week later in the small white church on the bluff overlooking the sea at Roche Harbor. The Bendiksens were there, Emma proudly holding Jamie throughout the short ceremony. Laurie was pleased to see Dr Finney and his wife in the tiny group, along with Joe Folsom and a few other island friends.

Except for short businesslike conversations to discuss their plans, she and Miles hadn't seen much of each other during the week before the wedding. She had been busy closing up the house and getting Jamie's things together to take to Emma's, and Miles had a lot to do to get the boat ready for their honeymoon trip.

Their honeymoon trip, Laurie thought sadly now, as she stood beside Miles listening to the minister pronounce them man and wife. What kind of honeymoon would they have when they had both entered into the marriage out of a sense of duty?

Emma had insisted that she let Carl take her down to Friday Harbor to buy a new wedding dress, and now she was grateful she had finally given in and done so, even though at the time it had seemed impossible to work up any enthusiasm over the idea.

She had chosen a simple silvery blue silk linen dress that sharpened and highlighted her clear grey eyes. It had a square, low-cut bodice that hugged her waist, then flared out in an A-line to just below her knees.

She knew she looked her best, as a bride should. Her black hair fell in a shiny cap around her tanned face, and although she wore little make-up, she knew her skin glowed and her eyes were bright.

She was especially glad she had taken the trouble to look her best when she saw Miles. At her first glimpse of him that morning in the church, she had almost cried aloud at how handsome he looked. She had never seen him in a business suit before, and with his immaculate white shirt and dark tie, he looked impressive and authoritative, almost forbidding. The deep aquamarine eyes gleamed in his deeply tanned face, and his dark hair was neatly combed.

Great spasms of love and longing shook her now as he bent to slip the plain gold ring on her finger. Then he looked at her, straight into her eyes, his expression unreadable. He kissed her lightly on the mouth, and they turned to face their guests.

They had planned to get as far north as Nanaimo on Vancouver Island that first night, then cross the Straits of Georgia and cruise aimlessly through the inland waters until the weather turned cold. After they had left Roche Harbor, waving to the little group assembled at the dock, Laurie went down to the main cabin to change into more suitable boat wear.

'You go ahead,' Miles had said with a little wave. He had taken off his jacket and tie and rolled up the sleeves of his white shirt above the elbow before they started out. 'I'll get us out into the straits, then you can steer while I changed.'

Laurie had hesitated, watching him as he concentrated his attention on manoeuvring the large boat through the narrow channel between the islands. The wind blew through his hair, ruffling it and plastering his shirt up against his chest so that it billowed out behind him.

She had longed to go to him, to say something to him besides the courteous impersonal platitudes that had been all their conversation for the past week. As if sensing her gaze on him, he had turned and their eyes had met briefly. Laurie thought she detected a gleam there, but he had immediately turned his attention back to his navigation.

Now, down in the cabin changing, she heaved a sigh of frustration. On her shopping expedition in Friday Harbor, a sudden impulse had made her buy a very brief string-coloured bikini, the first she had ever owned. As she tied the skimpy bra securely in front, she regretted the impulse. It seemed too much like a brazen invitation in the face of Miles' cool distant manner towards her.

Then she shrugged. What difference did it make?

It was the only bathing suit she had brought. She put a short terry-cloth robe over it and zipped it up. The robe only came to the tops of her thighs, but it looked demure enough.

She took the helm while Miles went down to change, and once again it was all she could do to keep from reaching out to him when he came back up on deck a few minutes later clad only in dark bathing trunks.

When he reached in front of her to take the helm his arm brushed lightly against her breast, and as she moved quickly away, her bare smooth leg came in contact with his hair-roughened one, and little sparks seemed to dance between them at the touch.

'Would you like some lunch?' she asked at last.

He smiled briefly at her. 'That sounds good. And a beer, too. I've stocked the fridge.'

Laurie went down to the galley and made sandwiches. While they ate, they chatted amiably, impersonally, and Laurie sensed a slight thawing of the stiff atmosphere.

'I think I'd like to get back to work at the bank right away,' said Miles. 'As soon as we get back to Seattle.'

Laurie gave him a quick look. They had never discussed the future before. She wondered if this meant he would start travelling again and if it was his intention to get away from her and Jamie as often as possible.

'I see,' she said. 'Yes, I imagine you must miss it.'

'How will you feel about living in Seattle? Leaving Cadranelle?'

She thought of the little room at the Barclay, the noise and traffic, the dirt, the crowds. What she wanted to say was that she could be happy anywhere Miles was, if only he would love her, but she knew she couldn't.

'I won't mind,' she said at last.

'You'll like it when you get used to it. Actually, I don't live in Seattle. I have a comfortable house on the water at the northern tip of Vashon Island. It's a little more populated than Cadranelle, but the atmosphere is similar. It's a short commute for me by ferry into the city.'

'You'll probably be travelling a lot anyway,' she said evenly.

He turned and gave her a look of surprise. 'No,' he said. 'I'm changing jobs. I'll be working at the main office—permanently.'

She waited, but apparently he was not going to elaborate. She cleared away their lunch things and offered him another beer, but he refused.

'I'm driving,' he said with a grin, the first light note in his tone for days.

Laurie caught her breath at how the smile lightened his sombre features, the bright flash of his teeth against the tanned skin, the graceful curve of his shoulder as he tossed his head.

'I think I'll stretch out on top and get some sun if you don't need me for anything,' she said, hardly able to bear looking at him, he was so beautiful.

He nodded. 'Go ahead.'

Laurie scrambled up the metal-runged ladder to the top of the boat. It was protected by a low railing and covered with padding, specifically designed for sunbathing.

She slipped off her robe and lay down on her back. She was already well tanned, the sun wouldn't burn her now. As she stretched, relaxing to the steady throb of the motors and the gentle movement of the powerful boat through the calm sea, she realised how tired she was from the strain of the past week and all she had had to do to get ready for the wedding and the trip.

She closed her eyes, thinking of Miles and wondering what kind of life they would have together. She would try to be a good wife to him, to fit into his life, so different from her own. Gradually she drifted off to sleep.

She woke up briefly some time later. It seemed to her that the motion of the boat had stopped, that she could hear the sound of the anchor chain being dropped, but decided she must be mistaken. Nanaimo was a fairly busy harbour even in the off-season, and there wasn't a sound of other boaters to be heard. Laurie closed her eyes again and slept.

She was awakened by the most blissful sensation around her midriff, a gentle stroking that reached from the upper edge of her bikini bottom to the lower edge of the bra. She opened her eyes.

'Miles,' she whispered. He was kneeling beside her, bending over her, his chest bare, his dark hair falling over his forehead, his eyes fastened on her outstretched form in the scanty bathing suit. He smelled of salt air and clean perspiration and the faint yeasty odour of the beer he had drunk at lunch.

He raised his gaze from her body to meet her startled grey eyes, and the look of hunger and longing in his face matched her own.

'That's a pretty eye-catching scrap of bathing suit you've got on there, Mrs Cutler,' he said in a low voice.

Mrs Cutler! Laurie's heart raced to hear that name on his lips. Then, conscious of her near-nakedness, she started to rise up, but he smiled at her and shook his head, forcing her head back down on the mat with a gentle, but persuasive kiss. His lips lingered, his tongue lightly outlining the curve of her lips, teasing, tantalising her until she was afraid she might moan aloud with delight.

Then he lifted his head and slowly, deliberately untied the front of the bikini top, pushing aside the scraps of material that covered her, his eyes devouring the full breasts that ached under his searching fingers. He leaned down and kissed first one hardening pink tip, then the other, his hands all the while molding the soft fullness beneath.

He reached for her shoulders and pulled her up so that she was facing him, his eyes glittering with desire, and pulled her to him just closely enough so that her breasts barely touched his chest, moving his upper body slightly so that the smooth skin of his chest rubbed maddeningly against her taut nipples.

At last she could bear no more. 'Oh, Miles,' she

cried, and threw her arms around him, pressing close to him in a frenzy of desire.

The gentle teasing was over then as he crushed her to him and his mouth came down on hers, plundering and invading. He leaned forward so that she was lying on the mat again, his body half on top of hers, his hands frantically moving over every curve, until finally they slipped underneath her bikini bottom.

He managed to free himself of his bathing trunks without leaving her, and then he was on top of her and she cried out with joy as they reached the heights of love together.

Later, they lay side by side, naked, her head cradled on his shoulder. The sun had just set and dusk was falling.

'Miles, where are we?' Laurie giggled. 'Not at Nanaimo, I hope, or the other boaters must have had some unexpected entertainment!'

He chuckled deep in his throat. 'No, not Nanaimo. We're in a little cove at Salt Spring Island.' He turned to her, drawing her to him. 'When I got a glimpse of you up here in that ridiculous bathing suit, I headed for the closest place I could find that I knew would be private. I wasn't going to let an opportunity like that go by on our wedding night. But I'm warning you right now, that outfit is for my eyes only. It's fit only for a husband to see.'

Laurie shivered a little in the evening breeze. It was growing cooler now that the sun had set, but the coldness in her stemmed from a different cause.

The passionate lovemaking with Miles had satisfied her body, but her heart was aching with frustration, and confusion. How did he feel about her?

Oh, he desired her. That face was unmistakable, and if he had married her out of a sense of duty, then at least she was glad she pleased him physically. But was that enough to build a life together on? She shivered again.

'Are you cold, darling?' Miles reached for her robe and slipped it over her shoulders. 'Why don't you go below and see if you can put a meal together for us? I want to check the anchor line again.'

Down in the main stateroom, Laurie took a quick shower and slipped on her yellow shift over her bare body. She debated putting on some underwear, but in a little flash of defiance, decided not to. If all she could evoke in the man she loved was passion, then she'd make a good job of it. After all, she was on her honeymoon.

Still, as she stood at the galley sink putting a salad together for the dinner, she couldn't choke down the feeling of sadness that pierced her heart. She wanted Miles to love her. Once she had thought he might, a year ago, when he had first come into her life that stormy night on Cadranelle, but so much had happened since then, and they had hurt each other so badly, that it was probably too late.

'Do I have time for a quick shower?' Miles called to her from the top deck.

'Yes, of course. There's no hurry—it will keep.'

While Miles showered, Laurie fumbled idly with

the salad, her mind on the dilemma that tormented her. She stared blindly out of the round porthole, hardly seeing the beautiful secluded cove where they were anchored, the moonlight cutting a wild golden swathe through the still water, the towering trees that loomed protectively on the nearby island.

I've got to offer him his freedom, she decided at last. A silent sob caught in her throat. I love him too much to hold him to me just because he thinks he owes it to me.

Then she heard his footsteps coming down the companionway, and he was behind her. His arms came around in front of her to hold her. She looked down at the strong forearms around her waist, the silky black hairs that covered it, the long tapering fingers that gently slid up around her ribcage, and she felt desire begin to rise in her again.

'Mmmm,' she heard him murmur. His face was buried in her hair now, his hands moving along her slender frame from her waist to her hips.

Laurie opened her mouth to speak, but could only gasp as she felt those roving hands settle firmly on her breasts, gently kneading. She felt his own breath quicken as one hand slipped inside the low neckline of her shift.

'What have we here?' he murmured in her ear as his hand circled the soft flesh, his thumb gently stroking the hardening tip. 'Braless, Laurie?' he went on in the same teasing voice, his fingers sending shafts of fire through every part of her body. 'For shame!' and his other hand began to undo the buttons.

She was speechless then, lost in the overwhelming sensations his touch aroused in her. She watched, mesmerised, as he pulled the shift back off her shoulders and the strong hands came back to take possession of her breasts again. Then, as one hand slid down over her stomach to her thighs, she couldn't stifle an audible moan.

In one swift movement, Miles pulled her around to face him. His mouth came down on hers, hard, demanding. He tugged at the shift until it fell to the floor.

'I want to look at you,' he breathed, his eyes devouring her. 'I can never get enough of looking at you.'

Then he lifted her in his arms and carried her down to the stateroom. He laid her gently on the bed and she lay there watching as he straightened up and removed the towel that had been fastened around his waist. He lay down beside her and raised himself up on one elbow. He looked down at her, his hand stroking the smooth black hair back from her forehead.

Laurie bit her lip and looked away with a deep sigh. How could she ask him now if he wanted his freedom when she loved him, desired him, so much? He was so dear to her that she could hardly bear to look at him.

'Why the long sigh?' he asked, lifting her hair and nuzzling gently under her ear. 'Feeling a little shy of me after all these months?'

She shook her head. 'No,' she whispered, 'it's not that. It's just that . . .' She could feel the tears threatening. 'I hate the idea that you married me out of a sense of duty.' She still couldn't look at him.

She felt him stiffen and draw away from her. Then he took her chin in his hand and forced her head around so that she had to face him, to look into those deep blue-green eyes, widened now in shocked surprise.

'Duty?' he echoed unbelievingly. 'Duty? I love you, you little fool!' He gathered her to him, and she slumped against him, throwing her arms around his neck.

'But you were so cold all last week,' she said, shuddering against him. 'So distant.'

His hold on her tightened. 'I was concerned about *you*,' he protested. 'I didn't want to rush you. I knew that one touch, one kiss, even one word of love, and I wouldn't be able to stop.' He looked into her eyes. 'I've loved you since that first night when I came dripping and battered to your front door. From the moment I saw you in that silly bathrobe, trying unsuccessfully to keep it closed while you stitched up my arm, I knew I was lost.'

'Oh, Miles,' she breathed, pressing herself up against him, revelling in his male hardness, 'me too. I love you so much. I've never loved anyone else.'

His hands moved gently over the curves of her body. 'How could you ever doubt I loved you, you idiot?' he murmured as his mouth brushed lightly down her throat.

She drew back from him a little. 'I was so afraid

you only wanted to marry me because you felt responsible for me and Jamie.'

He raised his heavy eyebrows. 'I *do* feel responsible, but give me credit for knowing the difference between duty and love.'

'Oh, I knew you wanted me,' she went on, her fingers playing idly in his crisp dark hair.

Miles raised his head then and kissed her hard on the mouth. 'You're damn right,' he growled against her lips. 'I want you, I feel responsible for you, and I love you beyond all reason. Okay?'

'Okay,' she murmured happily, reassured at last.

'Then quit tormenting me, Mrs Cutler, and let me prove it to you.'

And he did.

# INTIMATE
# MOMENTS

This Romance selection entitled 'INTIMATE MOMENTS' is a new selection we have introduced due to the large demand for our gift packs.

The special feature of 'INTIMATE MOMENTS' is that it contains four titles which we are publishing for the first time in paperback, the four titles have previously only been available in hardback.

As this is a new pack, we would like very much to know what you think about it, so please spend a few minutes completing the following questions, and in return we will send you a FREE Mills & Boon Romance as our thank you.

Don't forget to fill in your name and address, so that we know where to send your FREE book!

Please tick the appropriate box to indicate your answers ✔

**1. From where did you obtain your 'INTIMATE MOMENTS' selection?**

Mills & Boon Reader Service ☐

W.H. Smith, John Menzies, Other Newsagents ☐

Boots, Woolworths, Department Stores ☐

Supermarket ☐

Received as a gift ☐

Other (please specify): _____

**2. If the pack was a gift, who bought it for you?**

_____

**3. If you bought the pack for yourself, what was your main reason for purchase?**

_____

**4. What do you like most about the design of the pack?**

_____

**5. What do you like least about the design of the pack?**

_____

6. **Would you like to make any other comments about 'INTIMATE MOMENTS' selection?** _____

7. **Have you previously bought or received any other Mills & Boon gift packs?**

   Mother's Day Pack ☐          Holiday/Summer Reading Pack ☐

   New Author Pack ☐            Mills & Boon ☐
                                Romance Christmas Pack
   Temptation Christmas Pack ☐

   Other (please specify): _____

8. **How many Mills & Boon Romances do you read in a month?**

   Less than one a month ☐      Five to ten a month ☐

   One a month ☐                More than ten a month ☐

   Two to four a month ☐

   Other (please specify): _____

9. **Which of the following series of romantic fiction do you read?**

   **Mills & Boon:**                    **Silhouette:**

   Romances ☐                           Desire ☐

   Best Sellers ☐                       Sensation ☐

   Temptation ☐                         Special Edition ☐

   Medical Romances ☐                   Summer Sizzlers ☐

   Collection ☐                         **Zebra** ☐

   Masquerade ☐                         **Loveswept** ☐

   Gift Packs ☐                         None of these ☐

10. **Are you a Reader Service subscriber?**      Yes ☐      No ☐

11. **Are you working?**    Full-time ☐    Part-time ☐    Not working? ☐

12. **What is your age group?**
    16-24 ☐    25-34 ☐    35-44 ☐    45-54 ☐    55-64 ☐    65+ ☐

# THANK YOU FOR YOUR HELP

Please send to:  **Mills & Boon Survey,
P.O. Box 236, FREEPOST,
Croydon, Surrey CR9 3EL**

Ms/Mrs/Miss/Mr _____ IMOM 1

Address _____

_____

_____

_____ Postcode _____

mps
MAILING
PREFERENCE
SERVICE